By *the* Waters
of Whitechapel

BERNARD KOPS

By *the* Waters
of Whitechapel

W · W · NORTON & COMPANY · INC ·

NEW YORK

ISBN 13: 978-0-393-33737-2
Library of Congress Catalog Card No. 75-103966

Printed in the United States of America

1 2 3 4 5 6 7 8 9 0

FOR ERICA

By *the* Waters
of Whitechapel

1

Whitechapel appeared more squashed than usual. The poky side-streets all seemed pinched together. Nevertheless Aubrey was pleased to be home.

Bournemouth out of season had been as much as he could bear. Even the deserted Commercial Road seemed quite jolly in comparison to that graveyard.

They walked at a funereal pace through the smoggy morning, Leah stopping every few yards or so to blow out, breathe in, and to clutch at her heart.

Some mothers had the decency to die between sixty-five and seventy. But then, she was not just anyone. She was Leah the Feld.

Aubrey knew why she liked to walk the mile to Hessel Street. It would put her into her mood of happy discontent for the rest of the day. She loved to mourn her shrinking silhouette in shop windows. Her face was either tilted up towards her invisible god, or it was nodding down at the pavements where her ghosts seemed to cram each inch of space just beneath her own minute height. Only the dead seemed to appreciate what Leah had to put up with.

She started muttering to herself again, so he smiled and gazed beyond her, his vision towering above the mongol houses that squatted in rows along the decaying streets.

"If only you did not depend upon me, Mother." This time he spoke directly at her. The days when he feared this woman were as dead as the East End of London. But all she did was to continue her inaudible dialogue with her own dead.

They were nearly home now and when they reached Christian Street he took her wrist. It was no thicker than the neck of a chicken waiting for the plucker.

"Aubrey! You're stopping my circulation."

He released her and the usual sickening depression descended upon the world, covering his whole doomed domain. Three skinny neurotic pigeons pecked at the cold concrete. "Look at those nebbich pigeons," he said. Then he forgot all about them. "Mother—" he would allow himself the luxury of just one moan— "Mother, what is the meaning of me? What is my raison d'être?"

She looked concerned, "Don't worry, dolly—soon be home."

They turned the corner into Hessel Street. Aubrey could see their pathetic little sweet-shop at the other end.

"Why do you make me work for you? Have I been such a bad son?"

"Do you want my honest opinion, or the truth?" Leah laughed.

He pretended that she had not spoken. "I want my life to bear fruit," he answered, opening his hands in the manner of his ancestors.

"At thirty-nine you should be driving a wife mad and not your mother. At thirty-nine."

"Thirty-five!" he hissed back. "If you don't mind."

Then he decided to be compassionate. How could anyone expect a silly old woman to understand the blazing dreams of youth? "I do love you, Mother, but your life is nearly over."

[8]

"That's what you think," Leah replied with satisfaction.

"I must start thinking about my future," he said.

"Shut up," she snapped.

So he did; and it was a pleasure.

By now they stood outside the sweet-shop, which should have been shuttered. Aubrey could understand his mother's sudden concern. After all it was not only a question of the stock within, not just jars and jars of sweets on the shelves and the stacks of cigarettes. Beyond the shop and above it was their home. Everything they possessed in this life existed behind these walls.

"Someone's inside! Someone's inside! Get the police." Leah's frightened voice cut through his meanderings and through the noise of the Pakistani opera seeping from the house next door, as it had done, without a break, since the autumn of 1960.

She pushed against the door. "Should be locked. Shout for the police," she screamed as the door opened and the doorbell pinged.

Deep in the gloom of the interior he could see Auntie Beattie; economising with the electricity as usual.

"Who's there? Who's there?" Leah took up a full jar of sherbet lemons and held it high above her head, with shaking claws.

"Hello, Auntie Beattie," Aubrey said, switching on the light.

"Leah—why you back so soon? Thought you were staying a week." Auntie Beattie's melancholy voice was enough to reassure Leah. She replaced the jar of sweets and seemed glad that her sister had not seen. This was hardly surprising since Auntie Beattie could barely see her own five fingers if she held them up close against her own nose. Still, despite acute myopia, she handled the till all right. As she always said: "Money's like neon. It lights up."

[9]

"Didn't you like Bournemouth? I told you not to worry about the shop."

"I'm so glad to see you here, Beattie." Leah went behind the counter and the sisters kissed, each leaving a scarlet cupid bow on the other's cheek.

"Course I'm here. Where else should I be?"

Leah sighed and nodded and sighed and so did Beattie; sighing was the Esperanto of the Jewish race. In the hierarchy of primitive Yiddish sounds, the sigh reigned supreme.

Leah sat down behind the counter and took a mug of tea from her sister's flask. "So how's business? Taken anything? Ain't it lovely to be home, Aubrey?"

She was always like that, never waiting for a reply.

Auntie Beattie was pouring out a cup of tea for him.

"No thank you, Auntie. No thank you."

But she still pushed the drink towards him. He didn't want to hurt her feelings so he started sipping it.

"So I did right, eh? Opening up? You're surprised. Admit. How could I rest if my one and only sister was losing all her customers? So I did right?"

"You did what I expected you to do. But why no customers?"

"What's a sister for if she can't look after a sweet-shop? Specially when you had to go away to the coast to stop your highly-strung son having a nervous break-down."

"How dare you imply such a thing?" Aubrey stomped out of the shop and into the even gloomier living-room beyond.

"Hope you soon feel better, Aub," Auntie Beattie shouted after him and then her pink clean face came round the door, her mouth was opened wide and she laughed and laughed.

"Shut up. Just shut up." He shot away from the blob of flabby flesh and closed his eyes.

"I'm so pleased you're better. So delighted you're

behaving civil at last. You don't seem the same boy. Keep it up, please God."

He looked round and hissed.

But she was waving. "Toodleloo. Have a rest." Then Beattie returned to Leah and they continued the autopsy on the dead morning.

He watched them for a while through the open door. People said there was a great family likeness; certainly there was not much to choose between either of them. They were both bloody ugly. But then, it was his own flesh and blood so he was naturally biased.

"It's good to be home, but I'll die without tea. Can't understand. No customers? Not a single customer?"

"I put nothing in the till, believe me. And I put nothing nowhere else."

"Beattie! Please! How could you say such a thing? Would I think such things about you?"

"Na! Only joking. So what happened? Why did you come home?"

"Must make tea." She was about to hurry through into the kitchen but she turned to her smiling younger sister. "You're a good girl, Beattie. A girl in a million. I hope you don't leave me for the rest of the day. I couldn't manage otherwise."

Leah scooted through the living-room. "Tea with lemon, Aubrey. You'll feel better."

There was a sudden calm, and he opened his eyes, feeling totally unafraid of this room where he had been born. Yes, he, Aubrey Field, had actually fallen out of the universe into this ridiculous little existence via Leah Feld. He had grown up here behind these walls and played dark and light games and grown out of shoes in this very living-room.

He had not been born upstairs in bed like other people, up above the cracked stained ceiling where the flies were making love. Leah did not have time to get to the bedroom. "For once in your life, Aubrey, you were in a hurry. You couldn't wait." She said this over and over again, "You just couldn't wait."

"Wonder why?"

He did not wipe away the tears that assembled in each eye. It was probably onions anyway, if either his mother or aunt were peeling some, which was not unlikely.

He looked beyond Leah in the kitchen. No, he had never been convinced that he knew the entire story concerning his origins.

He looked beyond the house, beyond the street outside the window, beyond the world where a boat was wailing somewhere along the pea-soup river.

Beyond-beyond. To places without names and ideas without words.

Then he remembered that his toenails needed cutting. So he cut them.

Completing this satisfying task, Aubrey was disappointed. He loved the sound of nail flying in all directions and he wondered if just one piece had managed to reach as far as the kitchen and hit her just enough to remind her that he could wait not a minute longer for tea. Then he closed his eyes and decided to let everything flow over him. But when he opened them again, Leah had deserted the asthmatic kettle for the shop.

Leah stopped counting the stock and looked out at the lonely street.

"No one's about," Beattie said, leaning over her sister's shoulder, pushing her pebbled glasses right up against the window glass.

"No one? You should live so long," Leah ridiculed. "It's thick out there, with ghosts, memories!"

Beattie went back to the security behind the counter, but Leah continued talking. "They never leave you alone. Ghost dustmen; ghost coalmen; ghost beigel women; ghost schnorrers; ghost bubas. Then suddenly you realise you're all alone; everyone you knew or didn't want to know has been shlepped right out of the street and taken for a ride to Marlowe Road Burial Ground, East Ham, London E. 17."

"Mother, don't be morbid. Be miserable if you like—"

But Leah hadn't heard him. "Funny! As you walk along you see all the faces from the past. People you never lowered yourself to talk to, you now accept. You even cuddle them. You're glad and grateful they don't look right through you. You invite them inside for a little bit of homemade cheesecake. But of course —they can't come."

"Good job too; price of cheesecake." Beattie was used to Leah's sudden journeys into the unseen world of yesterday.

Leah came back down to earth; which was almost a fact, considering how thin and rotten the floorboards were. "No one about? Good job you can't see proper, Beattie. It's thicker than a flypaper out there. You can cut through with a breadknife." She laughed and then laughed at herself laughing and returned to the hub of her universe.

In the kitchen she made tea. "Think we'll have a nice drop of lokshen soup, later," she called to her sister.

"Just as well I bought a boiler, eh? It's in the fridge." Beattie lit up for having done the right thing.

Leah gave Aubrey his glass of lemon tea and then opened the fridge. "Lovely bird; it'll make a lovely drop of soup."

"Your soup never varies, Leah. You make the best chicken soup in London."

"For once I must agree with you, Beattie. I admit I'm good at many things, but nothing can touch my boiled fowl. I'll put it on soon." Leah smiled back.

Aubrey couldn't stand the conversation a moment longer so he went into the sweet-shop and opened a lucky bag.

It contained three minute cubes of dolly mixture, which he swallowed without chewing. He found a little plastic plane in the bag so he hurled it into the dirty sky above Hessel Street, forgetting to open the window. It nose-dived and lay crushed under Auntie Beattie's rather eccentric-looking plimsolls.

Aubrey opened the window to enjoy the final item the lucky bag contained: a party hat in pink and pale blue. It fitted his generous head so he kept it on and looked down Hessel Street, eyeing either end in turn, like a Wimbledon spectator.

"Aubrey!" she screamed. "Your tea is waiting to warm you up." But when she saw the party hat she shook her head. "Why does an Aubrey happen to a good woman like me?"

Auntie Beattie watched the two of them as she popped one lemon sherbet after another into her mouth.

"Stop eating the stock, Beattie. Eating the profits is no good for teeth. Even false." Then she turned to her son, despatching a sorrowful little wave. "Haven't I done enough? Haven't I slaved enough for you? Can you complain? Haven't I given you everything you needed?"

He nodded his loving agreement but continued thinking. Life was very tenuous. Your skeleton followed you everywhere; like an understudy, waiting for you to break your neck so that it could take over.

Leah stood at the sink watching for a saucepan to boil, and like most other mortals she didn't realise how close she was to death. She could slip and her whole head could go right into that large saucepan of bubbling water and her hard-boiled eyeballs would turn

[14]

white and her tongue would peel. Or she could just as easily faint over the washing and her head go down beneath the foam. Someone so easily, so gently, could give her a little push forward and hold her head under foaming detergent.

"Why are you laughing?" Leah said. "What you got to laugh about?"

Aubrey dismissed his frivolous thoughts. Who in his right mind would want to drown his own dear mother in a sink of suds?

Yet he felt a certain compassion for people who needed to do such horrid deeds. For sometimes the world misconstrued the real motive. People would be quick to condemn him for releasing her from this tormented world. Who would try and understand that he was merely thinking of her? For was there really any point in her continuing to live in this cruel world of indifference, plague, and drunken driving? Did society care a damn for the aged? To what did Leah have to look forward? Senility? Kosher meals on wheels?

"So go to the table; or do I take the table to you? Let's all have a snack," she said, carrying packets, containers, utensils and plates to the living-room.

"You have. I'm not hungry," he replied, squeezing a black-head that wasn't there the day before.

"Beattie? If you're not busy serving you may as well eat," she called. "Just a snack."

Beattie trotted out of the empty shop. "I'm already sitting down," she said, sitting down, closely observing all the usual delicacies as Leah laid them on the table.

"Don't worry, Mother." Aubrey continued gazing out of the window at absolutely nothing.

"Worried? Who's worried? What you staring at out there? Day after day."

Beattie shushed her sister rather noisily. "So he's a bit meshugger. So we have to humour him and make the

most of a bad job." She would have called her remark
a whisper.

"Wish I was in my grave. Matter of fact I wish I
was dead," Leah replied, slurping spoonfuls of cold
borsht down her own thankful throat.

Aubrey turned to his mother and smiled like a photo.
"You know I'll always take care of you," he cooed from
far away.

But Leah wasn't listening to him. "Eat then, Beattie.
Don't you like it?" There was more threat than concern in her voice.

"Yes, yes. Of course," Beattie replied hurriedly.

"Eat then. Anyone would think I never give you
no food."

"It's very nice of you," Aubrey heard his auntie
reply.

"Yes, it is. But after all you are my sister. Why should
I leave you out? You ain't committed a murder or
something like that. Beautiful chopped herring."

Then Aubrey noticed something for the very first
time. His mother's jugular vein stood out prominently.
It was like an undulating river. Or a serpent. He
could not take his fascinated eyes from the fearful little
snake. One little snip, with nail-scissors, and all her
blood would gush out from her interior. And she would
be dead. But not unkosher.

"Perish the thought." He shuddered.

"Perish all thought. You thought too much. Eat
better." She looked down in adoration at the tribal
table. "Thinking will be your downfall," she added
during a voluble mouthful. "This new green cucumber is the best I ever tasted, even if I do say so myself.
After all, I made it."

Leah finished eating before her sister had started
and she stretched her skeleton and yawned contentedly
to confirm the well-being she was suddenly experienc-
ing. But then she clutched her head and heart and

[16]

grimaced as if she were exaggerating a smile. "Oh, I got pain everywhere."

He watched her without emotion. One had to stand back sometimes from those one loved. Perhaps she would really die during this spasm; perhaps she would fall down on the floor, go dark blue in the face and explode.

Aubrey did not feel ashamed of his thoughts. He knew that he personally would not harm a single strand of hair upon his mother's head. Of course he did not hate her, although she sometimes got on his nerves. As a matter of fact he was quite grateful to her. After all, she had done her best for him, and once she even paid for tennis and driving lessons. He never really wanted her to die either by natural causes or strangulation. He had never done a single thing to be ashamed of as far as his sweet mother was concerned. Nobody could point the finger and say that he did not rank amongst the most devoted sons in the whole dark world.

Thoughts about her possible and imminent death merely arose out of his philosophical conviction that people should not be allowed to live beyond sixty-five. He personally welcomed the idea of being despatched by a helping hand before he approached the seventies. Anyone, but anyone, would be doing him a service if they pushed him in front of a train on the Central Line or sprinkled strychnine on his instant porridge.

But he was no dogmatic bigot. Other people probably had other ideas and they were perfectly entitled to them. There was no doubt that some people actually enjoyed living beyond sixty, and he was the first person to accede to their legitimate if ridiculous desire. It took all sorts—.

"Aubrey! Stop staring at nothing," Leah croaked, sucking up very slowly her own glass of lemon tea.

"Yes, Aubrey. You look pale. You've got a pallor.

If you must stare at something at least stare at the steam of the tea." Auntie Beattie winked intimately at her sister and nudged her. "And in an hour lokshen soup. One sniff of your mum's cooking and you'll surrender." She spread chopped liver over a slice of rye bread.

"My part. I should care. Forget him, Beattie. His own tea's stone cold and all the goodness is gone. But who cares? His funeral."

He decided to join them, so he walked over slowly and sat down whilst his eyes gazed up at the ceiling. It wasn't good to let your mother know just how practical and down-to-earth you really were. It was always imperative to hold the real you in secrecy and reserve. "So where's my smoked salmon?"

She laughed and twisted the flesh of his cheek. "I love your chutzpah. I've got some special for you." She trotted to the gas-stove to make him more tea and she hummed a tune that had headed the charts twelve weeks before. It was eminently forgettable but he remembered it because he remembered all things.

"Oh Mother," Aubrey spoke to air through the vacant smiling head of Auntie Beattie, "what is the meaning of me? What is my raison d'être?"

"Shan't be a tick," she called from the kitchen. "Don't get impatient."

"Impatient!" His lush resonant reply echoed through the entire house and was followed by a sardonic and iconoclastic laugh. "I want to escape. If only you would let me go. Mother, Mother."

"He's very clever. I always said so," Auntie Beattie said.

"Oh God, what would happen to you if I went? If only you would release me, Mother."

Leah hurried back and placed the plate of pink gold before him. "Thirty-five shillings a pound," she said, standing back to admire the best Scotch smoked

salmon, and her son, who cost her even more.
"Please. Please let me go." His voice was full of
compassion.
"He's so overstrung though." Beattie shook her
smiling head and went back into the shop.
"Eat up," Leah said, feeling his forehead, "and
later you can have a little doze. You need your rest."
Automatically he started to eat the delicious fishy
flesh. His hand and mouth were programmed for
delicatessen. His mind was free but his body belonged
to his ancestors; he was addicted to the necessities
that sustained them. It was useless, he was trapped.
She would never let him go.
"I've been thinking. We must discuss your future.
One day perhaps you'll leave home. One day, aluvi,
you'll fend for yourself. You'll go and stop driving me
mad."
He refused to listen anymore. She always spoke more
or less like this.
He uttered his loud and long sardonic laugh, the
laugh of a man sentenced to life imprisonment. If only
she really meant it.
Aubrey continued knocking back the not unpleasur-
able delicacy, moaning quietly between each devoured
mouthful, "If only you would let me. If only you
would let me go."

2

The day was not entirely a financial disaster. Auntie Beattie and Leah were soon busy dispensing packets of doomtubes to those who actually didn't mind paying for the pleasure of a painful death.

And quite apart from cigarettes, there were also the countless bottles of Tizer, bags of crisps, ice-lollies, jars and jars of sweets and dollops of petrified plastic called ice-cream.

Aubrey watched the customers from a corner, and he laughed. You had your choice. You departed from the salubrious Borough of Tower Hamlets from fatty heart, rotting mouth, or cancer of the lungs. Or, if you were strong enough, like Aubrey Field, you could choose your own method of suicide; or even die of old age, if you had that much patience.

A sense of calm descended over the shop as the money poured in.

The procession of kids edged slowly forward to the counter, but its length did not diminish. And when the children were actually close to being served, they thrust their arms ahead, as if reaching for Mecca. They all looked so scrubbed clean and their clothes were so spotless. A picture of bygone Hessel Street kids flashed to his mind. "Where are the snotty noses of yesteryear?" Aubrey intoned.

Beattie and Leah were taking money hand over fist, but their faces seemed more appropriate for the end of the world. "Every day's the same. No one. Then suddenly—everyone! All wanting to be served first."

But the sweating elderly sisters were equal to their task and coping admirably with the sudden rush of customers and heartburn.

In the gloom Aubrey boomed dramatically, "Never send to know for whom the till tolls, it tolls for thee."

"Poetry suddenly! It's foggy outside and he spouts," Auntie Beattie said, as she smiled across to her nephew to show she really didn't mind his special form of madness.

"Shut up, Beattie. And serve." Leah chided her sister and then bullied the sea of frail sepia faces beneath her: "I've only got one pair of hands! What do you want of my life? I'll stop serving altogether."

He wondered why she needed to complain. No one questioned her dynasty, nor her ruling rod of iron over her kingdom. She loved her position in the area, and she was as accepted and secure as Tower Bridge.

His mother had lived by sweets and she would die by sweets. Perhaps one day she might even have the good manners to choke on a bull's-eye. God forbid. But if she did, he had nothing to be ashamed of. He would throw a party for all the kids of the neighbourhood. It would probably even be reported on the front page of the East London Advertiser. With pictures.

He could just see her lying on a bed of coconut-ice, almost entirely covered with Smarties. She would love that.

And he would stuff a sherbet fountain into her mouth and stick two shiny black Pontefract cakes over her eyes. And he would use two splendid liquorice whirls for a moustache, and stick one red lollipop into each of her ears to give colour to her serene complexion.

And he would bury her like that, taking all the children to the cemetery, where they'd all play Postman's Knock, Kisschase, and Blind Man's Buff.

On the way to the burial and on the way back he would provide unlimited fizzy lemonade and crisps. And the children would sing merrily and wave at everyone.

He came back down to shop, where the queue had come to an end.

She had never escaped from E.1. and neither would he escape, and Hessel Street would still be standing long after all his mother's and his flesh had been picked clean by the better-class Jewish worms who had exclusive sub-contracting rights with the Marlowe Road Burial Ground.

A doe-eyed Pakistani doll floated into the shop followed by an avalanche of brothers and sisters. He knew the children well. They were all hooked on jelly babies.

What would become of these children? Would they escape from these streets where not a solitary tree had the chutzpah to grow? Would they ever discover that the sky was larger than a matchbox?

Probably! They'd make it somehow to Slough, Carshalton, or even Guildford. Everyone would escape this noose of streets, except Leah, Auntie Beattie and himself. Only the three of them and the lucky bags would remain.

"Come away from the open door, darling. You'll die. The wind comes straight up the river and turns left at Cable Street."

He stayed looking at the congealing sky, stroking his chin. "I think I'll grow a beard."

"When I'm dead, then you can grow a beard." She laughed and walked towards him, nodding.

Leah's face came right up close, like a zoom lens on television. She reminded him of a camel he once saw at the Bristol Zoo. She was a very nice beast and who could deny that he loved her dearly? She was his mother and deserved only the very best gratitude for all she had sacrificed from the day he had been banished from that horrible cosy dark womb into these dingy commercial outer-outer suburbs of Paradise.

"Without you I'd be free of you. After all, I do have my own life to live." There! He was at it again.

"So live it. There's the door. Outside is the street. One street leads to another. Before you know where you are you'll be miles away." She smacked him gently on the cheek several times, smiled and forwarded a pouted kiss.

"Oh Mother, how subtly you weave your spell." There was simply no point in trying to escape on such a cold day, anyway.

Leah went back to her counter, where her hands started moving back and forth, doling out packets and bags of pleasant poison. Aubrey followed her behind the counter, and stood with one hand clutching the richer sections of his hair.

Baldness would become him, would emphasise his uniquely high forehead. Anyway he would never be entirely bald. The grave, fortunately, would intervene long before anyone would guess that he was indeed much nearer to Yul Brynner than Samson.

"Anyway, if I'm so useless, why do you put up with me?" He hoped she wouldn't see his fingers crawling spiderlike, up one glass sweet-jar in order to extract a really delicious-looking piece of pink and white coconut-ice.

"So, Beattie, as I was saying about Bournemouth, the food was out of this world, but the waiters were from another world." When there were customers in the shop Leah just continued talking to her sister about life, death and rheumatism. She served them but ignored them. It was as if they were invisible until the time came for them to pay. "I put up with you because I'm your mother. Who else would stand for you?" By this time he had almost forgotten his question. "Who'll look after you when I'm gone? Mind you, I'll probably live longer than you," she continued, "Specially if you keep eating coconut-ice."

It slackened off later and Aubrey returned to his one and only hobby, watching the street.

A smell of joss-sticks hovered on the smoggy air, and this, blended with curry, made him want to hold his nose. Instead he pressed it flat against his face with the palm of his hand. Three black men passed. They were laughing at some private joke, their bodies bending almost to the pavement, which normally does not hear human laughter so close.

"Why shouldn't they laugh, considering what they're planning to do to us?" Leah said, once more joining her son at the door.

"All the new faces seem so unfamiliar somehow," Auntie Beattie sighed.

"Beattie! Shut up. And keep your eye on the till," Leah snapped. Then gazing at her son, lovingly, she shook her head to show that he just did not know the realities of the street. "Faces unfamiliar?" she ridiculed. "Only too familiar!"

"I do not understand you, Mother."

"With their eyes they don't need hands."

His eyelids flickered for a while and instead of speaking he nodded his head slowly.

"You're old enough, Aubrey, to face life, if you don't mind me saying so." Beattie held her mouth, hoping she had not spoken indiscreetly.

"They never leave a woman alone. Even me. And I'm not that young, am I? Mind you, I'm not that old. Am I?" No one confirmed or denied.

"Well, do you think I'm so decrepit that I still can't even be insulted? Sexually?"

Sister and son shook and nodded their heads so as not to make any mistake.

"What exactly do they want from me?" Leah asked all her ancestors in the sky.

"Well, it certainly ain't your intellectual equipment." Auntie Beattie laughed like a fishwife, and Aubrey was not surprised considering she used to sell herrings down Wentworth Street before her voracious appetite for a husband overcame her insatiable hunger for salted fish.

"A woman ain't safe in the streets nowadays," Auntie Beattie cooed.

"I should think you'd be perfectly safe, Auntie Beattie," he mumbled.

"So why didn't you stay on holiday?" Auntie Beattie slowly rolled her tongue over her cemetery of false teeth to extract loitering strands of chicken flesh.

"Aubrey pined for home. He cried bitterly for his bed. He got homesick, even after two days." He heard his mother spinning her traditional yarn, but he simply refused to look upon her face.

"Liar, I begged to stay and watch the wrath of the sea."

"You were such a lovely boy, Aubrey. Where did you go? I treat you like an eminent barrister, and you expect to be treated like ... the Queen's physician."

He pressed his face against the glass of the window. A child poked out its yellow tongue as it passed.

Aubrey could see the sisters reflected in the glass as they moved about moaning and clutching various sections of their bodies.

Why on earth were they still on earth? Why were they still wound up? Two dried-up pieces of leather like Auntie Beattie and Leah the Feld would have looked rather charming in a nice glass case in the British Museum.

There was something definitely not nice about the

[25]

old. Especially those who refused to move with the herd. Why had they refused to join that second most famous exodus in history—from Whitechapel to Golders Green? Why had they remained in the East End, which was now taken over by other scapegoats? Where was the treasure once buried along these streets?

"Where have all the Yidden gone? Long time passing. Where have all the Yidden gone, long time ago? Where have all the Yidden gone? Gone to Brent or Cricklewood—" His voice trailed off. One simply could not be ironic in Hessel Street.

"All right. There's the door, darling. You can get on a District Line train at Aldgate East. And if you change onto the Northern Line at Charing Cross, a train goes direct to Brent, Hendon and even to Edgware. Got your fare?" Leah smiled and opened her purse.

She survived by not moving. Like a fossil she soon became indistinguishable from the slums which had calcified around her. Every other Jew with self-respect had emigrated to North-West London, America, Israel, or the cemetery.

"Aubrey! You need a sleep." She was always a good judge of people in extremis, so he gladly re-entered the living-room. "Don't hate me, Aubrey. I'm all you got," Leah shouted after him.

"I want to do well. All the family did well. They died for instance," he shouted back.

Aubrey slumped into his armchair and breathed in blissfully. This was the only item of furniture that he would not burn when the Plague hit London again. He savoured the smell of pre-Hitler upholstery and he felt good.

Yes. The Felds were all gone and the Newmans were gone.

The future of the whole overstrung tribe lay in his unemployed scrotum. Dead and gone, all of them. Gone into the wooden overcoat or the mink overcoat.

Either way they were pretty rich and pretty high however low they had sunk. But whichever way you looked at it, they had all lost touch.

Everyone had gone and every white face had been replaced by a black face in Hessel Street. "Maybe that's what happens when you die. You come up again through a coal-hole all black in the face," he said to no one.

Aubrey thought of his father, which caused tears to congregate in his eyes. He did not stop them rolling down his face. Besides, they tasted rather special.

Then he thought of all the girls he once knew. Beautiful and succulent and moaning. Gone were the stinkfinger girls of yesteryear. Girls waving goodbye, with hands and titties wobbling out of train windows. Girls smelling of delicious sweat and cheap scent. Where were they, with their pre-deodorant pussies?

And where were the smells of Hessel Street? And the new cholas being baked for sabbath and the barrels of cucumbers being pickled? And lokshen soup and old prayer books?

"Mind you, I wouldn't say no to a girl with a deodorant-saturated pussy at this moment," he remarked to the pale photo of his mother's grandmother, who never stopped watching him.

He knew that his last remaining link with the past had gone. The smell of his mother's delicious chicken soup had been cancelled out by the smell of curry. And that eternal Pakistani opera poured through the walls of the house next door, sounding like a chorus of cats having a collective breakdown.

"Curry is not enough. They have to send us culture." It was just as well that Jews were a patient and tolerant people. He took up the broom and pounded the wall with the wooden end. "Shut up that racket in there," he shouted.

Leah came into the dark living-room and dusted the

[27]

wax tiger-lilies. "They've just offered money for the house—five thousand pounds cash. They even said they'd buy the business. Turn it into a Pakistani cake-shop. They can't wait for me to die so that they can fill every floor with sacks of rice and crates of instant cousins. On top of that they make it impossible for me to refuse by offering such good money."

"So what did you do?" He spoke slowly, his eyes closed.

"I refused."

She returned quickly to the counter. It was the place where she felt safest of all in the whole world of Whitechapel, but first she kissed Aubrey on the forehead. "I love you without a beard. Don't grow one. Look what happened to Bluebeard."

He watched her float away, and then within his closed eyes he saw another face.

The face of his father. First, in medium long shot; then cleverly zooming to a close-up for a benign, smiling love scene, which naturally was devoid of any suggestion of incest.

There was no doubt his father and he shared the same profile and the same dream; the dream to escape Leah Feld, considerate and lovable as she was. It was obvious there was nothing personal in his desire to free himself of his dear and only mother. Life was an intricate little pattern of paradoxes. Those you loathed you could live with forever. Those you loved were the cause of eternal pain. That sort of love had to be terminated with ruthless, selfless courage.

The curried air closed around him, but despite his despair Aubrey felt very happy. This inconsistency did not distress him; not in the slightest. Humans were made of far more complex material than even the Great Tailor cared to recognise.

3

═══════════

She was shaking him. He jumped up. He didn't know
where he was. "What? Why you waking me? Was
having such a nice dream." He pulled the blankets
right over his head and curled up, but that didn't
stop her. He knew she was still there.

"You were moaning. I heard you downstairs."

Aubrey threw the bedclothes off, then realised he was
in his own room, upstairs. And he didn't know if it
was night or day, or even what day it was.

"What day is it?"

"What do you mean, what day is it?"

"Why do you always answer questions with questions?"

"Me? Since when? So tell me why were you moaning?"

"What you talking about? I couldn't have been! I
was dreaming of my father. Is it morning or night or
just one of those days?"

He could tell she was about to perform. "When
they buried him, they buried not a man but an arch-
angel." Then she came back up to earth. "Aubrey—"
she looked extremely pained "—if only you took after
me instead of your father."

He turned over to stare at the more relaxing

wall. It didn't matter what day it was. Any day was every day, and every day was hopeless.

"What's the time?"

"What's so important about time suddenly? Catching an airship to Miami? Come down. The clock ticks down there."

He got out of bed and put on his pyjamas. But of course his mother had already left the room and was now mouching about the landing, thinking about prices wholesale and retail.

Aubrey always slept in his shirt and in his socks. After all, one never knew when the four minute warning would come. One could hardly be expected to rush to the underground station with bare toes.

But for decency's sake he always put on his pyjamas to go downstairs. He did not fancy presenting his aunt with new problems. In the first place Auntie Beattie was only human and overstrung. He did not wish to add to her burdens with thoughts of incest. One simply did not know what she would do next; and in the second place, people far less sexually demented than Auntie Beattie has succumbed to the coils of un-natural passion.

"What you don't have you don't miss." He poked out his tongue at the horrible yellow thing that darted in and out of his reflection's mouth.

He followed his mother on to the landing where she smiled at him. She smelled of mothballs and lavender and she stared with a slight smile poised tentatively upon her face.

"What you staring at, Mother?" He held her arm lightly, not wanting to be reminded of her surface frailty. She was a deep woman, full of symbolism.

"Just a fly that should have been hit with a rolled copy of The Times days ago." He clutched her bone with determination, and her enigmatic expression fell off.

"The Pakistanis will be signalling their Mosque in

Woking before you know it, and we'll be occupied, and have to teach them English. And how to eat sweets."

Aubrey could see her proper mood. Leah did this performance at least once a year. No one knew the exact cause. "If we still don't understand the lemmings, how on earth can we possibly understand you, Mother?"

"I sacrificed everything for you, Aubrey. Because I loved your father. I must have been crazy, and everyone told me I was, because he was no good, but I wasn't mad, so I entered into negotiations, which were eventually engrossed. So we signed our lives away. And you came. And you were enough. With you and your father I think I did my duty. He never came down to earth. To turf, yes! But to earth no."

"I know, Mother. Men are curiously planned."

They both entered into the gloom of the living-room.

"Let's go away, Mother. I mean somewhere further than Bournemouth. And let's stay longer than two days. I know, let's go to Calais?"

"You know I can't stand uncivilised places. Besides, the only way I'll leave this shop is in a box." She went out into the shop, smiling and nodding and shaking her head. "A mother is a mother," she said sadly.

He wondered if she was a secret Gertrude Stein or Anton Chekov reader. What on earth did she mean by her exit line?

Aubrey could not face the mirror nor the shock of the day, if it was day. For looking out of the window gave him no clue. The sky was neither here nor there.

He shlepped up an old quilted bedspread, lowered himself and settled back into the armchair.

The sounds of the sisters receded, and the sweet-shop seemed to be far, far away.

But Leah returned, thrusting something towards

him. "Have a beigel. It's fresh and lovely and hot!"
Then she faded back into the unreal distance again.
He took the beigel, bit a chunk out of it and threw the
rest away over his shoulder.

He would not succumb to the temptations of his
young days, when he used beigels rather than doughnuts under the sheets. They were somehow more proper
and less messy. However, even doughnuts, fresh or
stale, were preferable to using the hand. For that
method was unmistakably self abuse, and therefore rep-
rehensible. Besides, even beigels had been redundant for
a long time, owing to the neverceasing growth of his
now magnificent Goliath.

He had merely outgrown all that, but just this once
he decided to resort to his right hand and pray later.
He pulled his hot companion ever so gently, thinking
of various women and projecting them onto the screen
of his mind.

First of all the intelligent nude who had adorned
the cover of the intellectual Sunday supplement. But
she didn't work, so he rejected her and conjured up
Rita Cohen, a girl he had once been rather intimate
with. Yes, he remembered well those mad days when
he played hospitals with Rita. On his sixth birthday
she allowed him three fanny probes with his little finger
and he never saw her again. A recent eye-witness told
him that she worked for a hair-dresser in Cricklewood
and was still something sensational if you looked close.

But Rita as she once was also wouldn't work the
magic, and Goliath still showed no signs of getting up.
He pictured film stars, lady politicians and even a few
left-wing lady novelists. But nothing seemed to work,
so he put it away, and tried to think about other things.

He loved the old armchair even though the leather
was torn and it was falling to pieces. He rubbed his
nose into its guts.

The smell of the leather and the straw interior was

the smell of the past, the smell of his smell, the sweet tobacco smell of his father. It was the smell of security, of dark, lingering safety.

Often he had turned this armchair upside down, to hide beneath it, to hear them speak of him.

"That boy will be the death of me," Leah in the past said again and again. "The death of me. The death of me."

"Aluvi! You can do with a rest," he replied ever so gently.

Where did statements go, once they had been uttered? He wondered for a moment, then came up with the answer. They didn't go anywhere; they lingered for certain sensitive souls to pull them down from the dark ceiling stains in order to play them back once again.

"That boy is so gifted," his father said. "Why does my son turn out to be exceptional?"

Father was getting into his uniform. He was going off to Russia this very evening, to organise the Red Army for Trotsky.

"Naturally, Trotsky will get all the credit." Father was tugging his tight, long leather boots on to his rather splendid feet. Only boots of such obvious calibre were worthy to walk the Siberian winter.

"That boy will drive me to the grave," his mother cried, stirring and stirring the soup, adding garlic and tears.

"Aubrey is exceptional. He will go far." And these were the last words his father uttered before he left the house, resplendent in his cavalry regalia. "Aubrey will go far," he repeated loudly from the street he was already striding through.

"Not far enough," Leah replied. She didn't look down the street as neighbours came out to cheer his receding father who was going just as he came, stars in his eyes—the red star of Karl Marx in the left eye

[33]

and the golden star of King David in his right eye. Everyone threw red, white and blue streamers and confetti as they softly hummed the Internationale.

But Leah did not leave the scullery. She cried all the time into the food she was always preparing.

He never saw his father again. And even if he had died before Kiev, who was he, Aubrey Field, to stand in judgment of a hero of such stature? Anyway, his father was dead. Aubrey was sure. Solomon Feld was the dying sort. People with one golden eye and one crimson eye always were.

And Leah cried six or eight tears into the soup every day; you had to give credit where it was due. It was extremely unkind of him to believe she was merely trying to save a pinch of salt.

He could hear them squabbling again in the shop. Auntie Beattie and his mother were having an intense love affair. Arguments were their sole means of contact. The sisters needed each other's curses as other people needed a kind act and an encouraging word.

Aubrey turned the armchair upside down and managed to get under it without too much strain or overlap.

He knew he was not as lithe and bendable as he once was. You had to watch yourself, even if you had barely entered your thirties. His mind sauntered back to a few years before this day.

It was probably 1941, and he was about ten years old or eleven. He remembered it distinctly. But then again—why shouldn't he? Wasn't it only the other day when the sirens wailed and the bombs crumped and mortals descended into the underground? Every night they had to shelter beneath the streets of the city and Aubrey loved it.

"Why me? Why do they want me dead?" Leah cried skyward every time the earth trembled. "What did I do to them?"

One simply could not tell her that it was not the direct

[34]

wrath of Hitler and Göring that caused them to live in this deep-down world of carbolic and common humanity.

"Aubrey! He's got it in for us. Specially you and me," she said, smoke curling up from her red-stained fag-end. "Each bomb's engraved with your name and my name: Aubrey and Leah Feld." She licked her finger and drew their names in the dust of the platform. "That's why you mustn't let one single bomb on us. We mustn't give that monster satisfaction. Understand?" She shook his little limp arm. "Understand?"

"No, Mother." Then his eyes would close and he would sleep, all curled up on the noisy underground platform. It was beautiful beneath the soles of feet, the cemeteries, the worms and the roots of trees and all those crouching creatures who watched and waited, peeping up through grass or paving stones or floorboards and lino, ready to spring on their two hairy legs.

But he grew out of his socks, and the all-clear sounded. And time passed. Sometimes it passed right out, and sprawled out on the floor in front of you. But it passed. As sure as other people's lives. Time passed and passed.

"The monster didn't get us." Leah giggled as Aubrey waltzed her down Hessel Street on V.E. day.

They danced and danced, and the war was over. "Wonder why he never managed to burn us into clouds?" Jewish women of her sort had a special way of staring at the sky. They always seemed to be saying, "I've taken enough from you." Even though they sort of smiled. But she soon contributed a normal, non-Jewish smile, and even drank some Christian beer.

Later, with a slow solemn glide, she went along the street, doling out lollipops and bags of sweets and packets of Sir Walter Raleigh Coconut Tobacco to the thousands and thousands of hands and mouths turned upward and open towards her.

Later that day all London danced. And then they were all gone, the faces, the songs and the bunting. But Aubrey could not sleep so she took him to Victoria Park, which was totally deserted except for ducks.

By the lake she stood, and by the lake she cried. And by the lake he stood like a shlemiel, watching the sky lit up from all the fireworks and fires of joy. And no longer did he hear the blood-curdling call of the sirens, and he hardly ever travelled on the underground. But those tube trains came back sometimes like roaring red dragons, hurtling through his dreams, crashing towards him with innards full of green people.

Leah spoke, and he shot up. His thumping heart had missed a beat, but she was merely talking to herself in the shop; checking and rechecking the stock, jotting down instructions to herself. "Don't forget, Leah—running low on sherbet dabs and refreshers."

Aubrey laughed so that she could hear.

"You can laugh. The secret of selling is buying."

Aubrey laughed again. He felt so warm and beautiful.

"You can laugh. You'll never hear truer words. That reminds me. Aubrey! Phone Beehive tomorrow. We're running low on nougat." But he didn't respond. "All right! Don't. If we run out of nougat you'll suffer. It's your legacy that will go down the drain." Leah shouted with glee. Then she continued checking.

It was as if she expected the entire stock to be whisked away when she turned her back. She didn't trust the goods. As soon as she turned away, she'd turn right back again and start re-counting until a customer came.

Some little girls were giggling somewhere, and reminded him of the children who once played upon these pavements.

All baggy they were, as if wearing cast-off adults' rags that had been stuffed with newspapers and sawdust.

In those days streets were full of kids shouting and laughing and flirting and teasing and crying. How he envied them when he pressed his face against the glass! He wanted so much to join their games of Old Tin Can and Knocking Down Ginger.

"Go out and play," Leah nagged as usual for she could never see that they were too rough.

"They want me for sweets! They think I'll pinch some for them. Don't want to play."

"Go. Go out and play." He could still hear her nagging as she pushed him to the door. He could still hear himself sobbing.

She ought to have understood that he was far too fragile for them. And sensitive. It was before the war, after all. And in 1938 he could only have been three or four years old.

Aubrey opened one eye, and looked at his mother, who was quickly fanning her flushed face, employing every single finger. Why did she always maintain he was thirty-eight years old, or thirty-nine? What on earth possessed her to insist that he had been born in 1930?

He closed his eyes again and went back into the deep dark.

"True, I might even be a little bit older than thirty-two or three, or even four—But thirty-eight is ridiculous!" he reassured himself, silently, and felt better.

But in the darkness he could no longer conjure up those pre-cathode children. He could just about imagine the lamp-post where they used to swing around and around on a skipping rope.

But those children were gone. Gone forever. They hadn't even left ghosts behind.

There were plenty of ghost people. Adult ghosts were ten a penny in Whitechapel. Asthmatic, wheezing ghosts on crutches, sighing as they came towards you smiling painfully, begging with their eyes for a little bit of sympathy as they walked right through you shuddering, leaving you all damp and heavy and limp with the water from their eyes and the vapour from their sighs.

He would even have tolerated ghost children walking through the shutters of the shop and pinching acid drops or a half-pound box of milk chocolates.

But now there was no one. Just the sisters and himself, and not a living person in the shop.

He decided that he would have to make do with the lone pink image of that lovely living boy—himself, as he was before the war, when he was either three, or five, or eight. What did it matter? Nothing mattered now, for there was the lovely laughing boy that he was, tight curls smothering his head, eating a chocolate éclair, waving to him from a tram or bus or tube-train.

"Lo, Aubrey. How are you, son?" he cried, waving back at the child.

"I'm lovely, Aubrey. How are you?"

"Incredibly splendid, Aubrey. Goodbye, Aubrey. Don't get lost and worry your mother."

"Bye Aubrey! Lovely seeing you. Love to you and to all of you."

"Goodbye—Aubrey—"

And the sirens wailed again. The wolves of war were snarling at the door.

4

The wind howled across the river. It obviously did not observe the Sabbath of the Christian god.

Then it occurred to Aubrey. It was a Jewish wind and had taken the day off yesterday. Now it howled and howled, but sometimes it sighed. Yes! It was definitely a Jewish wind.

"Loan us half a crown, Mrs Spiegelhalter. Lend us half a crown." It howled.

"Mr Levine, I want you. Mr Levine, have I got a bone to pick with you?"

Many bones had been picked. Millions of bones of the Jewish dead. Natural or otherwise. In Whitechapel natural. Elsewhere unnatural. All the bones had been sifted and graded and rendered down. All the bones except his own, his mother's, and Auntie Beattie's.

"Believe me, have I got a pain in my back!" the wind now groaned. Was he awake or asleep? Or was he dreaming he was awake? What did it matter?

Even the barges complaining in the fog were worm-eaten tailors who once huddled together outside Black Lion Yard discussing bladder trouble, unemployment and Karl Marx. And sea-gulls shrieking over the Pool of London were aunts calling from windows in the sky; calling Dave and Shirley and Doris home to plates of egg and chips.

All dead. All were dead. All the Jews were dead. All the Jewish dead were wailing together, and making no bones about it.

"Must get away," he heard himself say, "from this Whitechapel burial ground."

The Jews did die here, one way or another. The spirit died. They came here to live and feed their young but still felt far away from nowhere they could name. And here they waited, beside the waters of nowhere. They hung their singing children up to dry, worked and slaved, huddled together in a great herd, developed thick hides, and sacrificed. Then they died exhausted, hunted and haunted.

And now they were gone. "The elephant and the Jewish problem." He stuffed four strips of Spearmint into his mouth, chewed them together and laughed.

There was no more Jewish problem. There were no more Jews.

"Hitler won the war! Hitler won the war!" The melancholic aunt-gulls shrieked high and low, but in chorus.

"Lend us half a crown! Pay you back, Shobbus." The contralto wind sighed deeply. "Mrs Spiegelhalter! Please spare me half a crown."

"Mr Levine! I want you. Have I got a bone to pick with you." The fat Yiddisher now soprano breeze fluttered over all other sounds rising from the earth.

In the other room, outside his dream, the till added its own funeral tones, each coin adding another farewell note to his own lost lostness. Until—

Aubrey was young again. Belly gone. His face no higher than the table-top, his head of hair a barber's nightmare.

The streets were full, because people came out of their houses in those days.

He was being led away by the Indian toffee-man who was taking him to India, where they would both live on Indian toffee. Day and all night for ever more.

"Why you taking me away?" Aubrey asked the ever-smiling milk-chocolate face that conjured perfumed pear-drops from eyes and mouth.

"I want whole of Asia to see how nice boy you are," the man said, spinning more and more strands of sky-blue pink sugar, and whisking fountains and fountains of Indian candy floss from his nostrils which floated straight into the gaping wide mouth of Child Aubrey beside him.

Then he heard his mother call the dark down, so the Indian toffee-man ran away, across the road, barefoot, carrying his shoes. He was soon lost in the crowd, and he was never seen again.

So Aubrey turned to his father striding along with heroic moustache and visionary look in eyes. Solomon Feld walked right down Mile End Road, applauded by all the tailors and furriers who continued arguing as soon as he passed.

Father marched straight to Aldgate East underground station and asked the booking clerk for a ticket to Kiev, where he had a pre-arranged meeting with Leon Trotsky and thereby he saved Russia from those reactionary hordes who attacked a few weeks later.

Aubrey waved at his father outside the Kosher slaughter-house, and his father waved back. Unemotionally; with his usual economy of movement, nobility of stance and dignity of expression.

When his mother dragged him all the way back to Hessel Street he was crying, for his father exploded in a sky bursting with streamers and candy-floss. "Never go with foreigners. He'll turn you into Indian toffee, take you back to Hong-Kong and pass you off as a darkie. They can even uncircumcise boys, so I heard. Don't wander off again."

"But Mother, it was Father, I had to say goodbye. All Russia was waiting for him."

He knew he was still dreaming, so he didn't crouch down when the synagogue exploded in Stepney Green. The debris made no sound as the shattered building fell all around him.

Families stood around roasting meat and chestnuts in the flames, but the chazen didn't seem to notice as he stood before the broken Ark, raising his silver goblet overflowing with the Palestinian wine, pitching his voice to the sky which was God's last known address.

Aubrey left the desolation and followed his mother past the Jewish Hospital, where sad faces of dead children peered from every window. Little hands waved slowly down at him. He waved back and he blew a bubble especially for them from his everlasting strip of bubble-gum. The bubble became so enormous that it filled the whole of Stepney Green and reached almost as high as the fingertips of the dead children. They laughed and laughed silently behind the glass.

Then he caught another glimpse of his father, galloping in the opposite direction. But he could not quite see the horse. His father's moustache was so grand now that surely God would be jealous and therefore claim him before the racing season ended. One day the wings of that moustache would rotate and Solomon Feld would soar up into the evening sky.

"Yes! Look! There he goes. He's waving down at us, Mother."

"I'm going to join Trotsky, to show him how to organise the Red Army," Father called down through a megaphone, but soon he was no more than a speck in the ever-congealing sky.

"Bring him back! Bring him back!" Aubrey called, but the Almighty was as jealous as the next man, or used ear-plugs. Either way Aubrey was most reluctant to blame God. There were terrible sounds around in those days. And shortages. "Are there soup kitchens in heaven, Mother?"

But his mother pulled him away from the shivering street and he never ever saw his father again. Except like now, in dreams.

Outside the school in Senrab Street he stood with her. The huge pram crammed with sweets that she was selling to the baggy children.

And as he spoke confectionery still rained down: bull's-eyes, toffee apples, gob-stoppers, chocolate kisses, lucky bags, liquorice whirls. And children were rushing everywhere, thousands of thin little white faces sucking, sucking, their clothes bulging with their surplus, which fell down their sleeves continuously and littered the whole of Mile End Waste.

Later Leah pushed the pram home.

"Maybe I need a brother in that pram, more than bull's-eyes!"

"You're too beautiful to be repeated!" she replied.

"Aubrey, Aubrey," the children mocked. "Aubrey! Aubrey! Fat little Aubrey. He's got silk gutkers on, and money in his pocket."

"Maybe, but my father and Trotsky are conspiring to change the world."

"Don't you ever have anything to do with Trotsky," she said briskly, pushing the pram onward. "You're better off without him."

He cried. She patted his head. "If only you weren't so innocent. So beautiful."

"Can you loan me half a crown?" the Yiddisher wind howled. Then it, too, curled up and died of cold. And the elements made no more sound.

"O Father, who art in Russia, send me back your medals, or a photo of your grave," he prayed.

He remembered how she screamed in Yiddish on that day, "A broch on his kishkers." He never dis-

[43]

covered if she had meant God, his father, or himself.

"Why do you cry when you curse?"

"To me, Yiddish is a holy language, too touching to speak," she replied, dabbing her eyes. Leah was taking him home from school. It was the first time he had gone amongst the barbarians. He cried and hated it and licked his bleeding knees, but soon she was taking him to and from school all the time.

Then he was going there all on his own.

He looked at his teacher. She wore tortoiseshell glasses and did not smile behind them. She just looked right through you.

It was November 28th, just after school had ended. They were alone on the stairs, Miss Levy and himself. Every detail was crystal-clear.

"You have the gift, Aubrey. You are touched by the gods, Aubrey. You can do anything, Aubrey. Anything. Any time. You will go far, Aubrey. You can go far, Aubrey. You should go far, Aubrey. Perhaps I'll give you private tuition, Aubrey. Come to my house, any evening you like. I can fit you in. Come."

Miss Levy was very nice, even if she did breathe heavily down her nose. Her face was close, desiring him.

He never went to her house. Maybe he should have been kind and given her the thing she most urgently required. After all, good deeds never went amiss. He had so much to give, so much to spare. But he decided against Miss Levy. He had no wish to hurt her. But what was the point in giving her a solitary glimpse of paradise if he merely had to withdraw it again? It was better for her to languish in her dark cell of hopeful frustration. Anyway, he had nothing to spare for her.

Leah turned her pram into a tuckshop and his father was a dead hero. But none of the kids believed the amazing exploits of his fabulous father. They even had the audacity to demand photographic proof. So he washed his hands and the past disappeared like dirt.

Aubrey opened each eye separately, and returned into the frozen curried air of reality. But he experienced no overwhelming desire to stand upright, so he slowly moved about on all fours, imagining that he was a lizard born before the beginning of time, before the invention of human eyes.

Then he got up and stretched and yawned. And yawned.

A wonderful thing had happened while he had been replaying his tapes of personal history: Auntie Beattie had gone home. He looked out at the violent purple sky. He longed for a miracle. Perhaps he would see his luftmensch father today.

He loved miracles, because they were few and far between. Infrequent beacons that threw light upon the darkness of the world, reminding people that people were not nice, and that goodness and justice did not prevail. It was always reassuring to face the prevailing darkness with such concrete faith.

In the empty shop his darling mother leaned over the till.

"Where would I be without her?" he asked himself.

"Nowhere," he replied.

He owed everything to this unique and beautiful lady who stood in his way only because she thought she might be right. Certainly he felt qualms and regret for what he was about to do, but he decided that he could not replace the breadknife. He would walk straight towards her and cut her throat; thus he would take away all her financial worries and all those interminable forms she had to fill in. No longer would she have to argue with that sadistic accountant who almost made her spit blood.

He held the breadknife behind his back and

[45]

journeyed the endless distance of twenty feet, to where Leah was bent in financial anguish. An old woman, especially his own mother, should not have to cope with such gigantic problems, not to mention such a problematic son like himself.

He stood right behind her. "You're worried, Mother. Poor Mother."

"Worried! Course I'm worried."

Never had there been so much compassion in his voice, "It's me, isn't it? I wouldn't wish myself upon anyone."

She turned but did not see the knife. "I'm worried about money," she said.

She was such a marvellous woman. She never once complained of the rheumatism which coursed through her brave little body.

Nor could he remember Leah once mentioning her frightful fear of dying from cancer of everything.

He knew she had to have both the pains and the fears. Those surely were the occupational diseases of mothers who lived beyond their term, not out of personal consideration but for the sake of exceptional siblings, who could not conform easily like the rest of the dross.

He felt very, very close to her. Already all his trivial, negative feelings were falling away. Only the best of her would survive with him.

"You're not worried about money," he replied.

"Who worries about money?" she ridiculed.

"Only those with it and those without it."

He would cut her throat beautifully. One straight stroke. Swift and deep. A kosher killing by a devoted son.

"Wasn't it Oscar Wilde, or Sholom Aleichem, who once put it so succinctly? 'The coward does it with a kiss, the brave man with a sword.'"

Leah seemed shocked. "Oscar Wilde! Please don't mention that name in this house."

"He was also human."

"Human? A man who leaves his wife and children you call human?" She slapped her face and nodded. "What you babbling about, Aubrey? You look funny." Then flickering her fingers, she indicated he should bend at the knees, just a little bit.

Aubrey complied and Leah felt his forehead. Then she smiled joyfully and turned away again.

Clutching the knife tightly again he prepared himself for the one final thrust. Yet still the voice of hopeless reason wanted to be heard. How could he stop it? Deep down he was as human as every other stupid person. But he decided to indulge his one strand of cowardly weakness, his one final last throw.

"Mother! One last question—"

"Last? Why last? You decided to be happy for a change?"

"Mother, you must let me go. I love you, cherish you and respect you. But I must have my freedom."

"Darling! One thing makes me different from other mothers: I don't particularly enjoy being one. Go. Now. And report sometimes. Look! Here's fifty." She opened the till, "Well, anyway, here's fifteen pounds and sevenpence ha'penny. Leave. It's time you left. You'll be happier and I'll be happier. We'll get on so nice when you're not here."

She was an amazing actress; this performance could have convinced the whole world. Only he could see through the subtlety of the act. If he so much as took one step into that foggy street, she would collapse into an emotional moaning heap. And she would never forgive him, and he would never forgive himself. "If I left, you'd never get over what you thought was heartlessness."

"Try me and see, darling." She opened the door

and the non-paying fog entered the premises. Then she hobbled away mumbling, "Sacrifice! For why? Ain't I a person in my own right?" Leah appealed to the news announcer on the television screen. "Only the other day they were talking about women and what they are, apart from the usual thing, in the House of Commons. We're also people, believe it or not. Go, Aubrey! I don't expect no reward. My reward is you going. I brought you up. You're up now, and you can walk. So—toodleoo."

He held the knife high above the back of her neck whilst a vision of Valentino came to him.

He would simply drag her back, rather gently, and pinion her to the floor by using soothing, firm pressure. But no force. Then, with utmost compassion and perhaps a few last words of respect, he would pull the breadknife sharply across the whole length of her soft neck.

"What you doing with that knife, Aub?" Auntie Beattie's voice hit him like a fistful of jagged stars. "You might have an accident. Knives attract lightning."

It *was* Auntie Beattie behind him. He could have sworn she had gone home.

And Leah turned round as he lowered the knife-edge. "Mother! I must have more money. You must raise my allowance. Look at me! I'm a shloch. I can't exist any more on handouts." He looked along the saw-like edge of the breadknife with expertise and calmness.

"But Aubrey! Darling! Your mother gives you everything. Her blood even, if you needed it. You don't want for nothing." The myopic eyes of Auntie Beattie were drowning in her predictable oceans, whose tides rose and fell, regularly and constantly. And he was furious. Anyone would think that he had not sacrificed almost his whole youth for his mother. Anyone would believe that he had treated his mother without respect and consideration.

"Shut up, Auntie! This is between my mother and myself." Now they would see he meant business.

Auntie Beattie's lip quivered and her voice became even more hysterical. "Why's he so touchy? What have I done to him? This a way to treat an aunt? An aunt like me, especially? Why's he so touchy, Leah?"

"Touchy? You telling me something? He's so sensitive these days you have to speak to him through a silk handkerchief."

Auntie Beattie went towards her sister, closer to the source of her solace, but Leah stepped back, sharply. "But Aubrey's right. It's nothing to do with you, Beattie. Stop interferring."

Auntie Beattie forgot she was in the middle of a fit of weeping hysteria and retreated into a corner where she slumped into the rickety wicker chair and gazed at them with her pale open and shut face. "You're my only family, and this is how you treat me," she said quietly through the fingers that covered her astonished mouth.

Aubrey faced Leah, head-on. Now she would see the determined fire in his eyes. Now she would realise that no power on earth could thwart him.

"Well, Mother? I'm waiting for you to agree with me."

"No," she said.

"No? Why not?" he pleaded. "What are you saving it for?"

"For a rainy day." Leah pushed a choc-ice into her mouth. Then, remembering her rudeness, she took it out again and thrust it towards him. "Choc-ice? Go on. It's lovely."

The choc-ice touched the tip of his nose before he shook his head with dignified rage.

"She's saving up for a rainy day," Auntie Beattie

repeated. At times like this she became a toneless echo of her older sister.

"A rainy day!" Aubrey shouted back with all the sarcasm he could muster. Then he threw the street door open. It was raining cats and dogs outside. In fact, it was one of the rainiest days he had seen for a long time. "I must leave you then. Now! For ever! And for always!"

She applauded with lit-up eyes. "At last, Aubrey. You'll appreciate me. You'll thank me for making you make this decision. But don't come to thank me in person. Not often. Thank me on the phone, you can always reverse the charge."

"You're doing the right thing. Thank God."

He had every intention of leaving that very moment, but the rain was very wet. But he would go. Without any doubt he would be gone as soon as the worst of the deluge was over.

He slammed the door shut. "You think you're being subtle. You think you have me for always. But I shall show you." He faced the face that had held him in bondage since the beginning of time. "You've always tried to take advantage of my better nature."

"Sometimes it's just as well," she remarked sadly, as she tried to release the breadknife from his grasp.

He returned to the living-room and put the knife beside the loaf of baked sawdust. Then he peered out of the fly-blown window, out at the steaming streets and pelting sky.

"I'm going to bed; for the rest of the day." His voice sliced through the air and he stamped all the way up the stairs.

He got into bed, but despite his loneliness his right hand could always be relied on to keep him company. So he held his own willing flesh, "A friend in need is a friend indeed."

5

Aubrey had watched too many dawns to indulge in the false luxury of hope. Night was somebody else's awful day on the other side of the world, and darkness was merely a device to separate one monotonous day from another.

And now a new day had arrived with predictable punctuality, but nothing new would happen. No one would come to surprise him, and yesterday would be exactly duplicated. Consequently, he did not react ecstatically when the first fingers of dawn stroked the dark hairy belly of the world.

But all was not despair. Something new could possibly happen this day. Perhaps he would be able to kill himself just after breakfast; spectacularly, by diving off London Bridge. Or by kebabing himself in front of an Inner Circle train, at the height of the morning rush-hour. "All is not lost, my boy."

But his optimism proved short-lived. Someone or other would be bound to rescue him just in time. For some incredible reason society could not abide you suiciding yourself. It was probably sheer jealousy. "We've got to suffer this miserable existence; why should you escape?" they were saying.

He descended towards the monologues of the two sisters who appeared to be talking to each other. A stranger could be excused if he thought that they were engaged in an involved conversation.

There was no point in prevaricating any longer. The rain had stopped and today was as good as any other day for chopping down the family tree. He put on his scarf and overcoat and decided to take a one way ticket to eternity immediately. Aubrey was about to leave the house and enter Hessel Street.

"Where you going this time of day? Without even breakfast?" Leah raced him to the street door and stood with her back against it.

"I'm going to kill myself," he replied with the sort of emotion people usually reserved for ordering poached eggs on toast.

She looked terribly concerned and he was glad. At last she was realising that he was a man of his word.

"Kill yourself? Aubrey! Did I hear right?" Her voice went up and up. "Aubrey! That's no way to leave home."

Auntie Beattie joined them. She smiled more than usual and smelled of lavender and paraffin. Auntie Beattie varied her smell almost every day. "Ah, don't give us that. He's off to a rendezvous. With a girl." She nudged her sister, "I told you, Leah. He's a dark horse." Her continuing nudges seemed unnecessarily forceful.

"I wish it was a girl. I'm not the sort of woman who thinks no girl's good enough for my boy. I'd pity any girl."

He watched his mother for a moment. This would be the very last time he would see her alive. "I am going to end it all," he said very slowly.

"Whatever you do, at least eat some breakfast. You can't do anything proper on an empty stomach. It's not nice." She scooted into the kitchen and returned with a pickled cucumber speared on a fork. She smiled contentedly as she watched him munch the offering.

"Leah! Whatever happened to that nice girl Aubrey took out once or twice? Every time they looked at each other I heard the school choir sing Psalm 150. And I could almost taste the marzipan on such a gigantic wedding cake."

"Beattie, pipe down." Leah tried not to shout.

He felt quite sorry for Auntie Beattie, even if she was a stupid, silly, interfering old cow.

"You remember, Aub. What was her name again? No, don't tell me. I remember—"

"Please shut up, Beattie," Leah hissed through clenched teeth. But Beattie, for once in a while, took no notice.

"Wait! She was a well-built, lovely girl. On the tip of the tongue. Yes! I know! Wait! It was Miriam. Miriam Smythe. Aub, what happened to her?"

Aubrey opened the door. "Oh, her! She petered out before she petered in. So long, you two. See you if we end up in the same place."

The ladies sensed there was nothing else to say, and no one broke the silence as he left the house, and entered the street for his last exit.

"Aubrey! Aubrey! I must tell you something." It was her voice calling him. He turned and grinned.

Her face alone had entered the cold world of White-chapel. There was no point in him not listening to her last words. All condemned people received and deserved this privilege. And God knows it would be hard enough on her, being condemned to live in a world without him.

So he waited. And while she blew her nose and cleared her throat he waited some more. He was in no hurry. The worms would simply have to queue up patiently.

"Aubrey! Here is my last word of advice. Come

down to earth. I know it's nice to live in clouds and imagine you're something you ain't, but remember, people without money shouldn't go to auction sales. Understand? And—listen to me, Aubrey, this is even more important. Never be ashamed of your origins and where you live. And always wrap up warm. Now you know everything, Aubrey. Go! Go now. I wish you luck."

He turned and walked away from the smiling face that oozed tears that fell and splashed upon the wet paving stones.

He was going far away from Hessel Street. He might have been born amongst these stones, but if there was the remotest chance of dying today, he certainly was not going to have his body lifted and fingered by the street sweepers of Tower Hamlets.

Yes, he would die with ease, for he had grown to maturity. He had reached that exceptional state of adulthood which few men achieve. All in all, he had nothing to complain about, even if that in itself was something to complain about.

He turned into Commercial Road, and sang in his usual sonorous voice, "Say goodbye to your airs and your graces, say goodbye to your pants and your braces, say goodbye to your birds and the races—"

Of course, there was still time to achieve mortal success, but what was the point? Everyone who knew him said he could go to Rome today and after a year return with his remarkably unique talent transmuted into one of the greatest baritone sounds in the whole of singing history.

Or why shouldn't he be able to take up the brush in Paris and astonish the whole art world, if he so cared? "Look at Gaugin and the breasts of his dusky maids." He spoke loudly for all the streets to hear and he certainly did not mind in the least when the two passing schoolgirls started giggling. If Paul Gaugin could pull it off, why not Aubrey Field?

And what about Vincent and Picasso, and Chagall? They too did not deny their compulsion despite their years. But what was the use? Who would appreciate him sacrificing a quiet life for the responsibilities of adulation? At least in the cosy, dark grave, no one nagged you to get up. You just slept in, doing nothing for ever and ever. And, best of all, you didn't have to be anything down there. Your mouldy clothes held no money or membership card to the Playboy Club, and your apologies for fingers held no steering wheel, no girl, no school diploma. Everyone was equal inside the grass door.

Yes, suicide still remained a distinct possibility. Anything was better than breathing and thinking and having to feel guilty about the misery of a sad, mad, sweet, and senile mother.

He walked towards Gardiner's Corner, passing street after street full of emptiness, past all the familiar dead faces that loomed Lazarus-like before him. Sometimes they waved from puddles, sometimes they cried in endless queues that stretched from the roadside right up into the low clouds.

And there were happy faces, bartering and bickering and arguing over philosophy, pogroms and pickled herrings. These faces contrasted sharply with the living masks perched on programmed bodies on their way to factories.

When he reached the junction he realised he was incredibly hungry. His mother was correct; it would never do to die on an empty stomach.

He could just see her at the autopsy as the coroner's words added insult to injury: "He had not partaken of any food that morning. And please, Madam, the beating of ... ahem ... breasts and the pulling of handfuls of hair isn't going to help anyone."

[55]

Aubrey thought of Oscar Wilde and his tribulations. And Aldgate East became the outer wall of a tyrannical prison, and the East End was the entire soulless world to which he had been despatched.

He had rarely gone beyond Aldgate East. Beyond here lay a world of infinite opportunity and he could not call to mind the last time he had dared to gaze upon the walls where freedom started. There had been no point.

He felt like conversation, but there was simply no one he could talk to—not a single girl, not a solitary bus conductor, not even the not exactly plain female assistants at the public library. One in particular came to mind and would have sufficed, had she not a perpetual gust of halitosis below her glasses.

He sometimes did catch a glimpse of wild young girls when they crawled out from their depraved cellars behind the Whitechapel Art Gallery—girls who would fall instantly for his iconoclasm and complexity. And even if some did have dirty feet, he could easily accidentally push the goldfish bowl over them as they entered his house at three-thirty in the morning.

Anyway, what was the point of goldfish? You couldn't have a relationship with them.

His belly would not stop grumbling. And it became sheer ecstatic agony when his nostrils received a sudden whiff of fish. Fish frying. Silver Jewish fish. He was damned hungry for anything but goldfish.

Two giggling birds with legs right up to their bums passed by. He closed his eyes and breathed the smell of them in.

He knew that their conversation did not contain one single reference to Kant. But he saw no reason why he should not follow them, captivate them and seduce them; incredibly.

He could just see his mother foaming at the till when he had each in turn downstairs on the floor, and then upstairs. How could a son explain the new morality, when he and his friends practised such a very old, yet delectable habit?

It would just be too bad for his mother, she would simply have to have a heart attack or walk into the Thames if he did not oblige by his own exit. He would say, "Dear Mother, I have decided to cheat the worms. Meanwhile, we are all having each other, for one calendar month. And, incidentally, the goldfish is dead."

But these were daydreams, and therefore not nearly as real as nightmares. Consequently, his joy was short-lived. He knew he could never take anyone back there. His mother he could just about explain away. His background and occupation would be impossible to live down.

Aubrey had to admit the awful truth, he was ashamed of his origins. He was ashamed of the house and the sweet-shop. He shuddered as he imagined himself explaining himself to the more fortunate inhabitants of the earth.

"My name is Aubrey Field, from Hessel Street and of Hessel Street. And I am just going home to weigh up four ounces of sugar babies because that happens to be my occupation. But between you and me, I munch five hundred jelly babies every day. I bite right through their belly-buttons."

He was ashamed—ashamed that his mother had never had the courage to move through the North-west passage for the far-flung acres of Brent and North Finchley. He was ashamed of not having a fast-moving red vehicle to carry him from nowhere in particular to nowhere in particular. He was ashamed that he wasn't a consultant or a barrister, or even an accountant or dentist. He was ashamed that he couldn't boast. And with all that shame, how could he possibly hope to impress anyone? So what was the purpose in continuing such a shameful existence?

[57]

Suicide seemed to be the only reasonable way out of his predicament.

So he whistled, because he felt gay again. "As my mother says, one door closes, another door closes." Aubrey laughed and he didn't care what lorry-drivers thought.

And his feet were suddenly taking him to the only logical place under the circumstances.

The Kosher Wimpy Bar! In Middlesex Street. Aubrey entered the neon interior where two-legged animals were devouring four-legged animals with a ravenous stare and a chomping mouth. Their hands and arms all round their plates, protecting their kosher portion of cow. Their eyes darted to and fro just like the final day at Wimbledon.

"Oh, it's wrong, so wrong, to eat the flesh of a living creature. It's despicable and unforgivable, and if I were not killing myself I'd become vegetarian," Aubrey mumbled as he munched the delicious preparation before him. "Anyway, why should I go to God as a hypocrite? I shall face him with a blood-stained conscience, and I shall expect no mercy, and maybe be forwarded to hell where the truly wicked reside."

Besides, heaven was pointless. It would be even lonelier than Commercial Road on a Sunday afternoon. Only Auntie Beattie would be in heaven, even if she did fancy her own nephew. Aubrey was sure God was broad-minded.

"Do you have a delicious banana split?" he murmured suggestively to the frenzied woman who was mentally adding up figures behind the counter.

When he stopped enjoying the delights of his subtle mind, he watched four nibbling secretaries. He could just see them marching along Whitechapel High Street, returning to their offices, all of them smartly swinging along in precise military step. "Left titty! Right titty, left titty—right titty. Cha—a—nge TITTY!

[58]

Right titty! Left titty! Right titty! Present TITTIES!"

Then he started laughing until it became uncontrollable, so he had to clasp his hand tightly over his mouth.

They sent back nothing in return except waves of aphrodisiac from their exquisite oceans of lust.

And then he saw her. She sat three places along the counter opposite him, sipping lemon tea. The imprint of her mouth was stained on the rim of the tumbler.

He inched towards her, not caring if anyone thought he was one of those creatures who lived by the balls alone. Anyone in his right mind could tell at a glance that all he wanted was to gaze down her dress and try to glimpse the garnet bumps which surmounted her soft, pink domes. But the place was crammed so it was impossible to get close to her.

"Excuse me. My mother just died and she always sat in this chair. Do you mind?" His inclined head oozed two tears, just for the little Jewish penguin who sat beside him. Aubrey wanted everyone excluded from the temple that surrounded her.

The little man shuffled away, seeming relieved that it was not his own mother who had suddenly burst.

Aubrey turned to the girl who was now beside him. He knew, he just knew, he could have helped her, but unfortunately for her, he needed her seat at the counter. So she would have to go.

"May I speak? May I say something of a personal nature?" he whispered right against her unsensational, unkissed ear, and did not wait for a reply. But he did notice that she had turned the colour of borsht.

"I want you, I want you to lie down on the floor under these seats—no one will notice—and I shall get on top of you."

She dashed for the door as if she had heard the sirens, and now he sat opposite the impossible, beautiful eyes, set in a moody noshy face. And he could bear the delectable growing pains between his legs.

This meeting would change his life, he knew, as he tried to spear her eyes with his gaze.

She looked at him briefly, but he was not one to be taken in by beautifully obvious pretence.

"Tell me, what is your name?" His hushed tones drew her amber eyes towards his own. And her eyes melted and coagulated as she trembled and took a bite from her sandwich, which now sported the radiant redness from her yearning lips.

"I did ask your name." He yawned slightly, as if bored.

"Why do you want to know?"

"I must know. Do you mind terribly if I sit here, opposite you?"

She shrugged and took another morsel of meat. "Do as you like," she said with apparent indifference.

The flesh was pink, and here indeed were truly exceptional and passionate ears.

How could she not have existed yesterday? Or even this morning?

"My name is Aubrey," he could see that she was preparing to go, and in a moment they would be lost to each other. He nervously snapped his fingers for her bill. And got it.

"Oh—you shouldn't." Her eyelashes fluttered like a berserk safety curtain.

He paid the bill with a confident right hand whilst his other fumbled in his pocket to find the exact amount he had left. His left hand re-entered the world very, very depressed.

"As a barrister I find these sort of places fascinating," he yawned and inhaled a gigantic gust of Mitsouko.

She seemed to grow taller. "Really? My name is Zena Conway."

Her voice had suffered a sea-change and she stood

before him, her titties almost reaching out to him, yearned to be fondled. They were scouting parties, going on ahead, warning the rest of her about an approaching enemy. In this case her breasts had brains and soon would be sending back messages to lower the drawbridge.

And her eyes, her beautiful, trusting, fierce, fantastic eyes, seemed to drink him all up. "Are you really a barrister?"

"Yes! For my sins." Then he stopped looking at her eyes and concentrated on the rest of her.

6

"Isn't it a luxury? Walking!" Zena gaily remarked as they approached Liverpool Street Station. The overcast day had lifted, and the moody English sky blazed with golden light.

"It won't last," he said.

"Oh, you're a pessimist."

"Who in his right mind is anything else?" he replied without looking towards her, not for any special effect but because he had the strong but absurd feeling that she would suck him right into herself and devour him. And he would have been disappointed to be proved wrong.

"I'm glad you're a pessimist," she said. "It's more mature, somehow."

He walked upon the new surface of the world where every grey alleyway suddenly seemed that it would lead to an orchard with no angels guarding the turnstiles with flaming swords.

"Live around here?" He threw the words with a casual disdain that would have made even Belgrave Square sound like a non-salubrious address.

She sighed deeply. It was not a Jewish sigh, just a sigh. But she did not reply to his question.

Outside the police station in Bishopsgate, he stopped walking, closed his eyes, and there she was, obligingly naked and revealing her pink yearning flesh that was without one solitary blemish from top of forehead to tip of big toe.

They continued walking slowly and silently for a while, then he repeated his question. "Zena! Tell me, do you live round here?"

"I'd love to live here, it's so romantic and mysterious." She sighed huskily. "I live between two worlds. Stamford Hill. Most people passed through. We stayed."

"Zena," he gazed at her gravely, "never be ashamed of your origins and where you live. Accept what you are and who you are. It's not your fault if you were not born in the lap of extreme luxury."

Then he saw a cab far down the road, on the other side, so he hailed it.

Both the gloom and the watery grave had receded. And he felt gay as he raised his umbrella high and shouted, "Cab! Cab!", even though the driver had already seen them, "Cab!"

He was pleased to have remembered that people with position and taste never shouted "Taxi." Small things mattered. He could see how impressed she was and he felt very tall beside her.

"You do not seem to lack confidence," she said rather sadly, obviously comparing him with herself.

"Me? Lack confidence? Good lord, no! Why do you say that?"

"Ah, no reason. It's just that everyone seems to lack confidence these days." Then she perked up, smiled and looked up at him with admiration.

The taxi had done a U-turn and was now before them.

"May I drop you somewhere?" he asked.

"Well actually I'm going to Bond Street to have my hair done," she replied.

"Fine!" He turned to the cabbie, "Bond Street, please."

Zena nodded her beautiful head.

"It's good to get away from the hustle and bustle of the Inner Temple. Sometimes I come down here to improve my knowledge of mankind. We have so much to learn from one another." He knew exactly how to talk to her. And with that right amount of indifference and interest to make a woman frankly crazy for him.

Aubrey nestled back into the upholstery. Taxis were so womb-like, so reassuring. "Zena, I have something important to say to you."

She smiled, but did not speak. Her pretty little erotic ears were waiting on his words. "I have taken quite a liking to you. You interest and excite me, Zena."

Remembering the early chapters of the Kama-Sutra, he had an overwhelming desire to kiss the lobes of those ears, but he suppressed it.

He would have to be patient and emulate those great heroes of history that he so admired. He would have to wait for at least another day or so before he crossed the Styx, by that far less used route, the return journey from death, to where Zena was waiting to be pumped into passion, and thus back into life.

He patted the soft hand that had never done a stroke of manual labour in all its days or nights.

"How warm you are!" Then he realised the hand was his own, but a modicum of nervousness was only to be expected under the circumstances. Then he patted her hand. "How warm you are," he repeated.

"Only now. I'm usually freezing, but somehow not at this moment. You know what they say, 'cold hands warm heart'." She giggled. It was the first time she had stepped out of character, but he did not wince. Clichés did not destroy her classic sensuality. He just

[64]

had to have her, proverbs and all. He could easily discard the proverbs later.

"I never feel the cold, I'm always warm like toast." Aubrey opened the window and noticed that it had started raining. A few drops fell into the cab and splashed her face. He leaned over and closed her window.

He dared not think of the things that he dared not think about. So he quickly changed the subject. "I would like to ask you a very direct question and you needn't answer if you do not wish."

"Ask me," she said.

He knew she was longing for him to touch her, but he desisted. He simply had to be different in her eyes in order to achieve the same hillocks that all the other swine tried so hard to climb. But he would succeed where they had failed. By slow and brilliant strokes, he would get to the top of her and surmount her, and then slide down into the warm valley beneath, where all her treasure was waiting just for him, in that pulsing, untrodden cave. In other words, within a few days he would push his angry Goliath right up her crack.

What had he to lose? Until Zena his life had been worth nothing. And what had she to gain? Only the thing she desired most to lose, unless he was mistaken. There was no point in beating about the bush.

He leaned towards her, but did not attempt to kiss her. "Zena, are you a virgin?" He used a compound of compassion and gravity in his question. Compassion in case she had been inadvertently raped in Golders Hill Park when she was seventeen, and gravity to show that the condition of her maidenhead, or lack of it, was of some concern to him.

She did not look shocked but replied slowly. "That depends. I'm not really sure, sometimes I believe I am. Why?"

"That's good. That's very good. I'm very pleased with you, Zena. You have the thing I desire most: honesty."

"I've never met a barrister in the flesh before," she said, and her words caused his temples to pound.

"The Law of God is sacred to me, that's why I took the Silk in the first place. And incidentally, you are sacred to me. You are beautiful but sacred. A person of my experience and sensitivity can only afford to indulge in sexual passions within the security and sanctuary of marriage. Apart from the morality, there is also the needless dissipation of vital energy."

"Oh Aubrey, it's so nice to meet a man who can control himself."

"I can for the moment, Zena."

She opened her sweet-smelling African crocodile handbag and handed him a card. "My father is a Kosher butcher. Here is our address."

Aubrey did not reply because they were approaching Ludgate Circus. Somehow he would have to slip out, and unfortunately leave Zena to pay the fare. But for the moment he was happy, for he still had her for the length of Fleet Street. How marvellous it would have been for both of them if he really could have had her, on the floor of the cab, suddenly, and be discovered by a herd of hungry reporters.

He could just see the stark headlines.

"Aubrey, you ought to join the S.O.S."

"S.O.S? Who's drowning?" he flipped back.

"It's a charity organisation. We're a group of ex-grads. A nice crowd, Jewish of course. S.O.S. stands for the SLIGHTLY OLDER SET. I was against the title. I wanted the M.M.M.—the More Mature Motley. You see we're more mature than other groups. No fashionable pop ideas for us. We indulge in exciting intellectual and cultural activities, besides collecting a fantastic amount for charities. I wish you'd join."

"Aren't you a little young for the SLIGHTLY OLDER SET?"

"Oh, I'm the baby. They spoil me and I love it. You mean to say you've never heard of us? Obviously you haven't been reading the Jewish Chronicle recently."

"I can see that any organisation needs a mascot, but I would have thought my age might have jeopardised my chances," he remarked casually. "After all, I'm hardly—slightly older, am I?"

"I would say you might just about qualify, Aubrey. You're borderline—but—"

Then he saw the Law Courts in The Strand. "I'm terribly sorry. The Law Courts! A waiting client."

He looked at his wristwatch, "Omni pasquia miamonides fugit," he boomed as he opened the door. "I must dash. Forgive me." But the car still sped along, so he tapped on the glass with a threepenny bit, and when the cab stopped he jumped out. "Forgive me?"

"Of course. Never keep a customer waiting. Please phone me." She leaned forward to show she meant it. "Please!"

"Fear not. I shall tinkle you sooner than you imagine."

"Aubrey, are you married?"

He shook his head slowly.

"Why not?" she said with incredulity. "Everyone who hasn't got problems should be married."

"Law has been my obsession, my sweet girl, and I must be sure. I could not give myself to anyone. I have my honour and my pride to consider. I have also been exceedingly busy. It is only recently that I have considered sharing my life with someone else. My flourishing practice practically runs itself now, so all in all one could say I am ready."

[67]

Her hot mouth suddenly kissed him. "I like you, Aubrey," she purred huskily. "Please phone me."

"Oh dear, I really must dash—and I don't seem—" he was going through pockets as he was tearing himself away.

"Don't worry. I'll pay. I'm going furthest."

He smiled benignly.

"And if you lose my card I'm in the book, under my father's name: Lewis Conway 'Kosher Butcher'. And please join."

"I'd love to join you, in any exciting venture. Groups normally bore me, but for you—I'd love to join."

"Groups bore me too, but you know what mothers are. They think twenty-five is two thousand years too late." Her safety curtains went up and down several times. Then they stayed up. And she sighed plaintively. He wasn't sure, but it could almost have been a Jewish sigh, in embryo.

He closed the door, smiled through the glass and mouthed benignly, "Trust me."

Then he turned to the cabbie, "Speed on."

The taxi whizzed away, and Aubrey held his hand high, in Maccabean salutation.

He had done right not to seem too eager. Jewish girls, like time bombs, had to be opened very, very slowly and with fanatical care, if one was not to be deprived of a lifetime of blissful liberties.

He went over to a newspaper vendor. "Evening Standard please." He offered four coins, "Keep the penny change."

"Yes, sir. Thanks, sir. And that'll be another penny. You're living in the past, sir."

Aubrey parted with his last coin, then he looked around to see which side of the road he was on.

As soon as he got his bearings, he strolled slowly in the direction of his home.

7

Only the day before yesterday he had met Zena, and here she was stark naked and groaning for more and more of him. And the whole place was full of steam and roasting heat as they splashed in the water together.

Aubrey felt so wonderfully relaxed that he could have stayed there forever, even if it was a public bath and Zena was not there in the actual flesh.

He screwed up his face into a Viennese contortion and emitted a perfect Richard Tauber pitch from his diaphragm: "YOU—ARE MY HEART'S DELIGHT —AND WHERE YOU ARE—I LONG TO BE. YOU—UUUUUUU—MAKE MY DARKNESS LIGHT—YOU MAKE MY DARKNESS—"

"Shut up in there, Gigli!"

The water was now getting lukewarm, so he took action. "MORE HOT WATER NUMBER TWENTY-THREE," he shouted. And for the first time he wasn't scared of the labyrinth around and even the cacophony of farts sounded almost melodious.

Aubrey continued shouting for more water, until the attendant shuffled along the wet tiles and complied by turning the handle outside the cubicle.

The man within was resurrected as the water poured

into the bath, gushing around his toes in a deluge of delight.

Since Zena, two days before, things had not stopped gushing around him and within him. His confidence was as apparent as his penis, which now poked above the water-line without a sign of that nervous break-down it had recently been threatening. Since Zena, Goliath had refused to sleep and had begun to make his presence felt more and more.

"Enough! Enough!" Aubrey screamed, and the man outside stopped the water. Aubrey inspected his arm. It was as red as best-quality Libby's tinned salmon.

He settled back into the bath and floated. And he cast his mind back to the days when he came to these public baths just to pee in the water and stroke it onto his face with one index finger. In those days he did not care to be reminded of the ocean, and in order to justify his journey he had to make at least the small-est gesture.

The zinc bath at home hanging in the small scull-ery reminded him of the coffin where one day he would compose himself to decompose. That zinc bath would have made quite a nice coffin, come the holocaust, but as a bath it was perfectly ridiculous. Goliath had to be restrained under the water for fear of Mother or Auntie Beattie walking through and colliding with it, thus knocking off the whole surface of bubbles. With his mother it would obviously be an accident or dementia, but with Auntie Beattie he would not be so sure, even though she invariably said, "I'm not looking. And even if I did, I can't see. And even if I could see, I've seen it all before."

He closed his eyes and thought of Zena again. She lay, partly submerged in water, looking up.

Only her nose, forehead, lips and eyes appeared above the surface. But lower down, her rose-pink nipples poked above the water-line. They seemed to have been elevated for prayer, like sacred observatory domes. They were a delightful feast to dwell upon.

And lower still, the gorgeous rippling vegetation, her dark, furry little map of India.

"Hurry up there, number twenty-three!"

"Porter, I tip well, so don't nag me." He closed his eyes again and thought of Zena.

So far he had not phoned her. He hated to be cruel, but far too much was at stake. Her. And again he conjured up her body, stroking every section that he felt vital to her well-being. Then she floated on the surface beside him, moaning with ecstasy, "Again! Do that again! Yes. That! Do it again. And again. Don't stop, Aubrey. Please."

All her petals were open and waiting to fall. "Be gentle with me, Aubrey. Be gentle. But don't stop. Do what you like. But be good. As long as you are an exceptionally passionate man."

"YOU'VE GOT ME UNDER YOUR SKIN! YOU'VE GOT ME DEEP IN THE HEART OF YOU. AND DEEP AS I AM, I HOLD THE BEST PART OF YOU—"

He didn't care a damn what his neighbours in cubicles twenty-two and twenty-four thought any more. He would leave them to their sordid hand drill and their two-inch surface of mortal scum.

He and Zena played tug-of-war with their tongues, then he teased and stroked both of her pleasure domes in turn. He had met her only the day before yesterday and here she was, her ears being kissed with an anticlockwise fervour, whilst he slid his hand down and down and down, and then up and up into her! And she was crumbling and erupting and groaning for the coup de grâce. "Aubrey! Do it! Do it quickly. But take your time," she whispered urgently. "I'm in your hands. Use me. I'm all yours. Do what you like to me."

"I cannot. I promised. We must be brave, beloved."

[71]

"I leave bravery to someone who cannot know the bliss of a barrister lover who also happens to be Jewish and unmarried. Aubrey, you have a special visa because you have come closer than any man to the frontier, closer than I ever dreamed I could travel. Take me all the way. Don't leave me in the provinces. Take me now!"

"LASHINGS MORE HOT WATER NUMBER TWENTY-THREE!" Then he whistled the Barcarolle.

The bath attendant was outside again. Aubrey knew because of the heavy breathing. "Time's up. I'll let the water out if you don't hurry," he shouted and pounded on the door.

"Probably an anti-semite," Aubrey muttered and hurried from the water and according to his usual custom threw clothes on to the still wet body. This was a conscious action that he adopted years before without harmful effect. It was just one other action to remind Aubrey that he was different from other men. The world only leapt forward by the efforts of the unconventional. Alexander the Great himself broke the rules by chopping through the Gordian Knot, and thereby changed the history of the world.

The bath attendant came toward the new Aubrey, his mouth full of no teeth and his open palm incredibly grained black. "Thanks, guv. Hope you had a nice barf."

Aubrey, looking towards the skylight, dipped in his pocket and relinquished a threepenny bit. Then he strode out of the steamy dirt disposal unit and whistled Offenbach all the way home.

"Slack," said Auntie Beattie.

"Slack. Slack. You would think the world was coming to an end, tomorrow," said Leah.

[72]

"Slack. Slack."

The sisters were intoning their oratorio for two tormented voices and tolling till.

"Christmas is gone. And so is Chanukah. And everyone's gone—meshugger. And all the money in the world has gone down the drain," Auntie Beattie groaned with pained satisfaction, then continued chatting to the tall Negro who just stared through her with his glassy eyes.

"Yes, dear. These chocolates I recommend. Eat them myself. All day. Just can't stop. What do you think of the terrible wind? It cuts right through you."

"Everything cuts through in the end, eh Mister?" Leah laughed, turned to her sister and screwed up her face.

Aubrey entered smiling.

"Look at him! Vinegar beer bottle."

"Hello Mother my love."

"You been drinking? Should be ashamed," Leah sadly shook her nodding head.

"Yes. I've been drinking Zenaspume." He smiled and refused to descend to their tribal level.

The far away West Indian suddenly awoke to the fact he was a customer. "Hey! Serve me."

"Don't look so miserable, son. Easter will soon be here. I've got the first batch of Easter eggs in stock. Thank God for my wholesalers." Leah became gay again. "Yes, thank God for Easter."

It was probably only three hundred and twenty more shopping days to Christmas, and after Easter there was Mother's Day to come. "Mother's Day seems to come almost every day, these days," Aubrey said. "And after Mother's Day, Buba's Day. And after Buba's Day, Doomsday, please God." Then Aubrey remembered his misery was almost over. "Mother, the end of the world, as we know it, started the day before yesterday."

"Great poetry," the Negro remarked and shrugged off towards the door. "I dig that crazy son of yours." He laughed down in his belly, but it went on longer than necessary.

"My boy crazy? You're the meshuggener. Don't come back. We can do without," she screamed down the street after him.

But the Negro was lost in conversation with a postbox. "Come the revolution man, we redskins stick together."

"He called you mad. He can talk." Leah returned inside. "How could he say such a terrible thing?" She went straight over to Aubrey who was staring at nothing. "And although he's not right, I admit, you *are* crazy. And if I didn't love you so much I'd hate you."

Then the strangest thing happened. Auntie Beattie locked the sweet-shop door and pulled down the inside shutter. And, stranger still, Leah did not scream at her for doing such a thing. Instead, she pulled all the electric plugs from their sockets, removed the cash from the till, then, grumbling, she stacked the takings into various denominations. Then she counted it, recounted it, and locked it away in the safe.

Then both she and her sister got into identical Astrakhan coats and stood ready to leave the shop.

"But it's only four o'clock." Aubrey stroked his mother's fur collar compassionately; senility was not a very nice condition, not even in your own mother.

"We're going to the Grounds, to look at my poor Sammy's grave. Today's the tenth anniversary of the day. May he rest in peace. Such a lovely feller."

Aubrey had imagined that Auntie Beattie would have wept all her tears for her departed husband by now, but she still managed to ooze out just a few more.

"But we haven't got time. Soon be our busiest hour," he pleaded.

"You can always find time for the burial grounds," Leah replied as calmly as she could.

"Especially for our own funeral," he nodded.

"Come on, Beattie, let's go."

The sisters linked arms and stood ready for the alien pavements.

But Auntie Beattie was still sobbing too much for her sister. "Beattie! Pull yourself together. Years ago you could cry down these streets. Now they think you've a screw loose. Indians don't cry."

"Pakistanis, Mother."

"Same difference. Ready, Beattie?"

But Beattie still cried and cried. "Oh Sammy, Sammy! Why did they have to take him? What harm did he do anyone?"

"The good always die young!" Aubrey remembered his Uncle Sammy was far from good, but on the other hand he was far from bad. Sammy and Beattie had been a devoted couple and there had only been one or two skeletons in the cupboard.

No, sin had certainly not been Sammy's big fault. His badly clicking false teeth were far more unforgivable. Aubrey felt sorry for his aunt despite the strange way she looked at him whenever they happened to be alone.

He touched her arm affectionately, "There, there, Auntie." But the sobbing did not subside, indeed it grew and grew until the floorboards shook.

"You going to put flowers on him?" he asked the bereft woman in a very nice way, but her hysteria didn't diminish.

"Flowers! For why flowers? Will flowers bring him back? There's no point in flowers."

In this one respect Aubrey was in complete agreement with the rest of his tribe. There was simply no point in flowers. They withered as soon as you turned your back. They died and started stinking. Except

[75]

wax ones. Fruit on the other hand was a different kettle of fish. You could eat fruit.

"Well, Aubrey—?" They seemed to expect something other from him than slouching in his chair.

"What, ain't you coming?"

"No. Cemeteries tend to make me feel optimistic."

"What! You expect us to go through all these streets alone?"

They could continue this sort of cry, and they would. It would rise into a wailing climax of invective, but from now on he would remain as silent as Siberia. After one final statement:

"I'm not going out in these clothes."

"So, you'd let your mother be accosted on the way to the cemetery." His mother nodded with pained satisfaction. "What's wrong with your clothes? Suddenly?"

"I refuse to wear them ever again." And then Aubrey realised he was removing the garments. It was quite impossible to stop himself. So he merely laughed and undressed.

She covered her entire face as he stood in front of them with nothing on except his purple-patterned shorts. Auntie Beattie pressed herself into a corner, like a child scared of the hand of an ugly relative.

"Don't let me see. Don't let me see. I mustn't see!"

"No. Bet your life you mustn't see. It would spoil you for ever. Anyway, you can't see even with your eyes open."

"Aubrey! Aubrey! What's got into you?"

"Love! A compulsion to escape through the tunnel of luscious lust."

"Meshuggener! Meshuggener! Should be locked away, you should."

Aubrey held his head high and he marched into the dirty backyard, where he sprinkled his discarded clothing with paraffin. And there, amongst Coca-cola and Tizer empties, his handsome body becoming soaked with the rain, and singing 'On with the Motley', he struck a match and set his mound of rags on fire.

Then he stood back to watch the smoke and the flames rising into the dirty, lonely, darkening East End sky.

"That's that! That is the end of that."

He went back into the house, where two wizened faces were clutched by four wizened hands. He sat down behind the counter and he lit a whiff.

Leah scuttled upstairs and was smiling when she returned. "Here, your father's clothes. I was keeping them in case he ever returned. But whoever returned from the grave except someone I don't want to mention. Go on Aubrey, put them on."

Lightning struck his brain, salt came to his mouth, and all the darkness of Whitechapel receded.

He buried his nostrils into the hopsack material of the trousers, into the deep enclosing woollen fibres of pullover and jacket.

He fingered the flamboyant, colourful bow-ties whilst he speared the air with the engraved silver-handled walking cane. "On guard, ghosts!" Then he danced around the room with silk crimson dressing-gown, and attempted, successfully, a clear ringing falsetto, "Oh my beloved Father—" Then he rubbed his cheek upon the beautiful pair of shoes.

It would be a pleasure to walk in his father's shoes. So he did.

All the way along Hessel Street he walked proudly, if slowly, between the sisters, clutching at a bony arm of each.

And he could not suppress his desire to be happy despite the conversation that was about to be embarked upon.

"Everyone's escaped. Either by hard work or heart failure to East Finchley or Hove, or by hard work or heart failure to any decent burial ground you can name," Leah kicked off.

"Soon it will be my turn. Not by hard work or heart failure or by going to East Finchley. But by the sorrow I get from where we're going now." Auntie Beattie smiled as she spoke.

"I'm not going anywhere. I like it here," Leah replied, as they reached the main road and slowly walked along it. "They can pickle me and put me on a shelf in Bloom's. They'll never go bankrupt."

"Where's everyone? It's dead," Auntie Beattie sighed.

"Inside the furnished tombs, watching telly, rehearsing for death," Aubrey replied.

He looked up and tried to catch some rain on his tongue, but it had just stopped. And so had the clouds and the sky. All he could see were the egg-boxes of the battery people.

People who were living on top of each other, layer upon layer upon layer. They took their rehearsals for death very seriously.

The sky was full of people and the earth was full of people, but there were no people in the streets.

Just the three of them, Aubrey, his mother and his Auntie Beattie, slowly progressing towards the cemetery.

8

Auntie Beattie had dropped her flowers upon the tombstone and they left the cemetery.

All the way home on the bus they did not speak, but every few minutes Auntie Beattie's whole body reverberated, as it was struck by the tidal waves of her tearless sobbing.

When they reached Gardiner's Corner they got off the bus and stood silently for a moment, a trio by the traffic lights facing each other, as if involved in some kind of magical ritual. Aubrey shrugged, nodded and yawned, and felt just like a probable great great grandfather from God knows where. Leah grinned and Auntie Beattie cried quite openly now. At the same time she smiled, but Aubrey could not bear such a sickening display of mock bravery.

He was therefore relieved when she walked away backwards, towards her own home.

Aubrey and Leah watched her go, and soon she faced the way she was going and then vanished completely. Swallowed up by the hungry, endless bricks that covered the whole new, soulless world that once was the Whitechapel of legend.

The happiness Aubrey usually experienced in cemeteries also departed. But at least Auntie Beattie lived a quarter of a mile from Hessel Street. It was a great distance for such neurotic sisters to allow to come between them.

Commercial Road filled him with the usual dread. The same sickening nostalgia covered the whole area and clutched it by its roots, after it had shaken every vestige of life from its surface. Except for the few buses snailing towards some destination, there were also a few diagonal people, walking against the bitter wind, and the glazed eyes of pub-crawlers, but these few desolate individuals made no difference to the dirge for a dead district, which floated from the alien interiors of public houses, issuing from incoherent beery voices.

"If we don't move by the end of next week I'll burn the house down."

"It's a bit chilly," she replied.

Aubrey walked away from her, very slowly, "I'm going." He crossed the road. "For ever!" he shouted.

"Where you going?" She stood in the middle of the pavement as if bolted there.

"I'm leaving you, Mother."

"Marvellous. Need any money?" She sounded really happy.

"Course I need money. I need money to live before I die," he replied.

"But where you going?" she shouted.

"Bloom's! Where else? That's the only place I'm going. Coming?"

"No, I feel like the Grand Palais."

He wasn't surprised. Special occasions, like visits to cemeteries, circumcisions or someone else's heart attack were invariably followed by a visit to the high Yiddish drama. Tonight was not going to be an exception.

She crossed over to him. It was very nice of her indeed to cross the road just to give him the money. She did have a certain kind of primitive courtesy.

[80]

"The way you said you were going, I thought at least it would be Brighton." Leah took his arm, "I also feel like some salt beef," she said, and Aubrey knew there was no escape.

It was so lovely in Bloom's. He felt wonderful, and looked incredibly handsome in the peach mirrors.

"How's business?" he asked a hovering manager.

"Mustn't grumble," the worried man replied.

It was always a pleasure to come to Bloom's for a last meal. Not that he was now going to eliminate himself tonight or even tomorrow. It was merely that every meal at Bloom's seemed like a last meal. There was such an air of intensity haunting the splendid palace.

When the dissertations and arguments regarding fish, flesh and fowl subsided, Aubrey ordered, and when the food finally came they ate portions big enough to satisfy a condemned man. No man alive could argue with such food.

"Mind if I sit down?"

Aubrey looked up for the owner of the smaltzy brown voice.

The smiling gent standing before them sat down before they had a chance to reply or take that first important mouthful. The man obviously used shoe-polish on his beautifully groomed hair.

Then Aubrey remembered the face. He took his first forkful of salmon. Of course, this Lithuanian Lothario had been fishing for Leah for at least seven years, but so far she had not even nibbled.

Aubrey sipped his lemon tea whilst the Yiddisher actor laddie rambled on about the years and where they had gone.

"So how did I know the East End was dying? Simple! Once, in the Grand Palais, you couldn't get no seats for all the salt in Siberia. Not even if you were King Fifth of England. Everyone bought seats for life.

And when they died, God rest their dear souls, these seats were fought over by relatives, children, grandchildren," the actor looked around, hoping that the rest of Bloom's clientele were listening to his interpretation of history. His eyes raped every single table in turn, but his hands were dead still, one clutching Aubrey's wrist very tight. "Then guess? Pinkt! Suddenly one day a solitary space appeared. Just one. But then tomorrow another one. Then another. Gone. Mrs Greenbaum, gone. Morry Frankel, gone. Schlomo Gurevitch. See what I'm getting at? They was going —you know where. Where no one else can go for you. Gradually in the audience there were spaces instead of faces. Until suddenly—Bingo! Legs eleven—gone to heaven. Shnorrers five—no longer alive. That's how I knew my East End was dying. Marry me Leah, while there's still time."

The actor's mad suggestion sent a shiver down Aubrey's spine and the actor released the numbed wrist.

Aubrey stood up. "Excuse me. I must go somewhere."

"The call of the wild," the old actor laughed deep down in his throat.

"Don't be long," Leah mouthed to her son as she cut into some steaming sugary lokshen pudding. "You took long enough," she snapped at the retreating, ever-smiling waiter who had slid it in front of her.

"Thank you very much," the waiter replied, "thankings you. My service is your command."

"A Cypriot boy trying to look like a Yiddisher boy," Leah said as her son left the table.

Aubrey went straight to the phone and dialled Her number.

"Hello?" Her deep expectant fruity voice held the greeting for almost five seconds.

"This is me."

[82]

"Who's you?"

"Who else? Aubrey!"

"Oh, hello." Her voice lost its sureness and he was glad.

"I promised I'd phone," he breathed.

"You sound different. More mature," she said. "I'm longing to see you." Then she giggled. And then apologised for giggling.

"I must see you tomorrow. I have decided to join the S.O.S."

"Oh, fabulous! Tomorrow we have a cultural evening. They'll be absolutely thrilled at the news. Phone later tonight for details. Can't stop now. I'm in the bath, actually."

"Ah, the femme fatale of Stamford Hill."

"Hardly. See you tomorrow," she crooned.

"Yes. I'll come in my Lotus Elan."

"Just as you like. Cars don't really impress me. Toodleloo." She clicked off.

He walked back to the table, and he cursed himself for committing himself needlessly about owning a luxury sports car. But it was too late now, so he stopped cursing and started wondering how he would be able to acquire a Lotus Elan within twenty-four hours, with just thirty shillings in his pocket.

Nevertheless he felt extraordinarily confident as he sat down again, and smoked one of the Lithuanian's cigars which easily could have been mistaken for a firework.

He snapped his finger at the Yiddisher Cypriot. "Garçon! Encore apple strudel, s'il vous plaît."

The waiter flashed his National Health teeth and rushed towards the clatter of the kitchen.

9

From the moment he got up he had concentrated upon remaining silent. And he was succeeding.

She questioned him, pleaded with him and ridiculed him. And all the time she pretended to be lighthearted: "Who are you, Aubrey? I don't know who you are anymore; but I'm glad because I like the change. But who are you?"

"Goodbye," he said, leaving the shop.

Leah was too astonished to reply. She did splutter, but no words came, and he was gone before all the invective from the back streets of Odessa could escape from her mouth.

He walked slowly along Hessel Street and did not look back in case she hadn't burst into fire. On the other hand, he knew that he loved his mother more than anything else in the world.

It was Monday morning and the sun was witnessing the birth of his new determination.

He chased a bus and jumped on. "Fooled you!" he said to the ferret-faced conductor who was obviously disappointed that Aubrey had not fallen upon his face into the gutter.

He got off the bus at Gardiner's Corner, and there he found a plastic palace that pulverised coffee beans, and called itself Stromboli. All that steam from the espresso machines was probably meant to remind the nostalgic cafe owner of the volcano where his parents had been spawned.

The neon lighting and the perches for sitting upon were obviously calculated to get you in and out as quickly as possible. Unless one was partial to eye strain, headache and a sore bottom.

Nevertheless, he entered, ordered and dared the beverage.

There was no one about except a rather sad female slave who had been desperately trying to catch his eye but had now given up the attempt.

Aubrey took out the cheque-book. This was his passport into a new land—a land which was all the more sweet because so few dared to cross its forbidden frontier.

Then he took out a letter which his mother had only recently written, an illiterate letter to Her Majesty's Inspector of Taxes begging for a little more time.

He had not posted the letter, not out of forgetfulness, not out of spite, but because this one particular communication contained Leah's signature, crystal clear. Aubrey now was proud of that Aubrey of the day before, who then had the foresight to imagine a tomorrow such as this. He toasted that other Aubrey with another steaming cup of whatever the concoction was meant to be.

He was sure she wouldn't mind what he was about to do, would understand and forgive him. If she had only allowed him to take on the headache of the money in the first place, this whole situation could have been avoided.

He felt incredibly calm when he took up the pen and poised himself at the point of no return.

He murmured up a prayer of thanks to the British Broadcasting Corporation. The technique he was about to use had been shown only a fortnight before during one of those incomprehensible plays without a beginning, a middle or an end. The play featured an unfortunate forger, but he had forgotten the name of the play and the plot. The only thing that remained indelibly seared into his memory was that single act of forgery.

He turned his mother's letter upside down. Her signature now was no more than an abstract pattern of lines and loops. He simply had to copy each stroke precisely. By doing this he would apparently be able to control the impulse to graft his own unmistakable calligraphy upon Leah's overstrung scrawl.

Then he wondered how much he would take.

Two thousand pounds seemed a very nice sum. It would make a nice start to a life devoted to finding oneself, and also cover the small items he would need to buy immediately, and after.

"Selah!" Aubrey was not surprised that he felt not a shred of guilt. But then again, this was really his money. His own flesh and blood had been deposited every Friday morning, without fail, since the beginning of the world. And something far more precious than his flesh and blood had been banked. All his dreams and years had also been locked away.

He did not hold anything against her, however, and he had no desire to smash her face in with a hammer simply because she had used him in such a manner. On the contrary, he felt a tremendous compassion for her. She loved him and could not know the implications of her actions.

"It's all for you. All for you," she would say, clutching the cash under her coat when he accompanied her every Friday morning to the bank. Later she would buy her fish and her chicken and her giblets and her smoked salmon along Wentworth Street, and they

[86]

would return home where she would feed him all the addictive luxuries for her own pathetic motives.

What was the point of Leah saving money? To pass it on to him to pass on to somebody else to pass on? She always said she loved the thought of having grandchildren. But he knew that each grandchild would be a nail in her coffin.

"If only you got married and had children." He could hear her voice even now, more urgent than the steam of the espresso machine which was erupting away quite nicely now for the nicer sort of clerks who frequented Stromboli.

He would be free by the action of his own hand this very day. He needed his money now. Urgently. After all, he was still absurdly young and if the world discovered a cure for slight baldness, there would be nothing that he could not face alone.

He was about to deface the virgin cheque, but now wasn't sure about the amount he would need.

To walk into a showroom and buy a Lotus Elan for immediate cash would arouse immediate suspicion. People with money enough to afford such a car rarely carried that much loose change. And he could hardly give them a cheque because he simply did not have a cheque-book in his name. Furthermore, he could hardly pass himself off as Leah Feld. Therefore he would buy a second-hand model of the same car. Apart from the fact that it would be much cheaper and solve all his purchasing problems, a car with a patina had audacity. It was far more chic.

A second-hand car was infinitely more desirable. "A used car! So be it."

Aubrey's hand did not shake as it took him across the Rubicon. And it was done. And it was done perfect.

He left the restaurant smiling kindly at the waitress, who had resigned herself to the fact that she would have to survive her long frustrated life without Aubrey Field. But then fate was cruel and he did not make the rules.

He did not leave her a passion message with the florin under the empty cup, but she would easily see how generous he was. He wondered what she would buy with the two shillings. Possibly paper hankies, or a hundred aspirin. Or maybe she would keep the coin to remember him. He often overtipped, not because he needed to be remembered but because one could not fight an extravagant nature.

He entered the bank and it was a pushover. The girls knew him well. He loved banks and their mystical commodity, money. He loved the smell of banks.

"Two thousand pounds, Mr Feld!" The young, newly married clerk raised her eyebrows as she read his offering.

"Why? What's wrong, Mrs Agar?"

"Oh, nothing, sir. It's just more than your mother usually draws."

"Yes. It is. I'm in a tearing hurry, Mrs Agar, to buy some chopped herring."

"I'll just see if we have enough so early before our delivery. Shan't be a mo. Excuse me, Mr Feld." She hurried away into the entrails of the bank.

"And the name is Field!" he said, but very quietly.

He was about to step into the future, as soon as the foolish girl had verified the signature. But meanwhile his heart was breaking the high-jump record, but not from nervousness. Good Lord, no! Simply from the sheer excitement of the whole thing.

The girl returned and she was smiling. Aubrey noticed that she had unfortunate skin. "Would you mind waiting just a few moments Mr Feld—we—just—we do not—cold for the time of the year, isn't it?" She showed him into a room which sported prints of early English schooners on the walls; and copies of glossy trade journals, which contained not one single picture worth remembering in the lavatory, or the dark. And Goliath did not so much as twitch from either wall or table matter.

"The manager won't keep you a moment," Mrs Agar said, hurrying away.

"What's it all in aid of?" He smiled to meet her smile, but she had gone back to her box of temptation.

The manager came almost immediately, briskly and smiling, with his right arm extended. He was a manikin of a man whom nature had smiled upon. Unfortunately it had been a very cloudy day. "Ah, Mr Field. How's your charming mother?" A gust of halitosis came from the scrubbed hole stuck on the spruce little clockwork body.

"Not so good today. That's why I've come alone." Aubrey was not sure if all was lost, and laughed nervously. Anyway, Dartmoor was preferable to Hessel Street, so there was absolutely no point in worrying. So he worried.

"Come to the point Mr Fish. Why have I been brought here? Is not my mother's credit good? Does she not have quite a nice amount deposited?"

Fish offered Aubrey an abnoxious brand of cigarette, and he seemed nervous.

"Your clerk, Miss—I forget her name—she told me you were short of cash. Are you? Has there been a run on sterling again today?"

"Good Lord no. We have the cash here, naturally. She was just being polite."

"I shall have to forgive her, seeing she's just returned from her honeymoon. Working twenty-four hours a day is hard work. Well Fish, where's the money?"

"Of course! Here it is; neatly wrapped for you." He offered the absurdly small packet and for the first time since Aubrey entered the bank, he did not hear the slow tolling of bells.

[89]

"Of course we know you. And trust you. It's just that we have to be careful. Two thousand pounds is a lot of money, especially to Mrs Feld who never withdraws money anyway."

"Oh! You believe that this is the only place we bank?"

"I am truly sorry, but please understand that it's in your own interest." Mr Fish backed to the door and opened it.

"Oh, I do understand and I appreciate it. Have you counted it out yourself Fish?"

The manager nodded gravely as they both re-entered the money shop.

"Goodbye, Mr Fish. I must dash now. Toodleloo."

The manager accompanied Aubrey to the door.

"Doing something nice with the money?" Fish tried hard to sound casual, "Speculating, I hope. Wish you'd come to me for advice."

"You could call it speculating. Great growth. Branching out. New places. Branches and branches. Can't stop once you start. Envisage Eldorado. But fear not, Fish. We shall continue to bank at your branch."

"I'm very grateful. And please convey my fond regards to your mother, and I hope she's better soon."

"So do I. Goodbye." He laughed uproariously as he walked away, and the little manager also laughed for a while before returning to the glass interior where clients and coronary awaited him.

It was done. By keeping his head he could keep his freedom. Aubrey snapped his fingers in the sky, "Taxi!" He patted the contents of his breast-pocket with optimistic joy, and settled right back into the cab.

"Where to?"

"Harrods. And wait there."

"Yessir."

Aubrey watched the East End slip away. He was

[90]

emerging from the past and now he'd dress immaculately for Zena and the Slightly Older Set. And after Knightsbridge he would buy a fast-moving vehicle, as long as the colour did not clash with his avocado-green eyes.

He did not glance sideways at the city streets as they flashed by, but looked straight ahead. He was already arrowing towards the future. Theseus was escaping from the maze, Orpheus was undead, Prometheus unbound.

10

====

They entered the Serene Strudel, an expensive kosher restaurant behind Baker Street, and he persuaded her to sit near the window, so that she could gaze at his Lotus Elan, parked right outside.

"Lovely car, as cars go," she said.

"I'm not overstruck by any sort. After all, it's just a lump of metal to take one safely from here to there."

"But it's cosy. I've been in far worse vehicles," she said.

"Really! Yes, I suppose it's not too bad."

He felt absolutely on top of the world when he remembered how he had taken those second-hand car dealers near Warren Street. He had beaten them down fifty pounds at least.

He lit two gold-tipped Balkan Sobranie and handed her one of them. Then he allowed the smoke issuing from his own mouth to be inhaled again via his nostrils.

"I'm pleased you're joining the S.O.S," she said. "Let's hope it works out."

"I am a great non-joiner and a great resigner," he replied.

"We're very exclusive and constantly being bombarded by requests for membership."

He sat calm and silent until the cheese, listening to her

fruity voice: "I've never met anyone like you. Most available men are nebbiches."

"I suppose some are destined to be unique."

He ordered Parfait Amour with his coffee. He liked asking for the way-out liqueurs. Apart from putting the waiter and barman in a flap it helped to epitomise his original character. "Yes! One of the good shipments," Aubrey remarked, holding the purple liquid up to the light.

"I suppose you've been far too busy to have a regular girl-friend." Zena threw those words away.

"At last. A girl who understands the problems as a whole. Please tell me a little about yourself."

"Yes! I do trust you now. I think I can tell you certain things." He squeezed her hand again. She squeezed back and gave him an immediate and exquisite pain beneath the zip of his trousers. "Will I be meeting your parents?" he asked casually.

"Any time you like. Now, tell me about your parents."

"My mother is—is an incredible woman."

"And your father—?"

He sipped a little more of the liqueur and cleared his throat.

"Don't speak if it hurts," she murmured, closing his lips with the tips of her fingers. Her nails were overlong and would have sufficed in Chinese opera. "You're very special to me, Aubrey."

"Zena! You've thrown me off my balance, and I'm terribly sorry."

"Don't apologise. In a way I'm glad."

The heat pouring from her had not yet caused waiters to throw windows open. She leaned her head sideways, smiling at him.

"With you I feel I can speak freely," he said.

"Please do tell me everything, Aubrey. Trust me."

"The waiters here are known as the Kosher Hus-

[93]

sars," he replied and they both laughed. The laughter trailed off and their eyes locked together. "Later, Zena, I'll tell you everything. Now I must speak about my father. He died somewhere in Siberia, having created the Red Army for Leon Trotsky. A catafalque of ice was his reward before bears devoured every scrap of him in Irkutsk. And Trotsky, his more publicity-seeking comrade, got all the credit for my father's genius. Even so, my dear Zena, it did Trotsky no good. Even he met his end by the K.G.B."

"I'm so sorry, Aubrey."

"So am I. But let's forget it. One does not weep for the brave."

"Who was Trotsky?"

"Someone who had everything, even exile. The only thing he was short of was an ice-pick. But his comrades provided him with one, in Mexico."

"How sweet of them. Aubrey—it intrigues me why a man of your position and intelligence, not forgetting your good looks—"

He cut her short. "I promised my father never to leave her alone until I was married. And I believe promises are sacred."

"How beautiful. Are you a good barrister?"

"One of the best." He yawned again.

"I thought you would be. Live somewhere nice? I bet you do."

"Yes, in that avenue with rather large houses between Swiss Cottage and Regents Park. In Avenue Road. There are worse places."

"I'm glad you're a good barrister," she said. "Aubrey, you've made me happy."

"I intend to."

"I'm so glad the reason you cannot leave your mother is not your own weakness."

He lowered his sad eyes for the weak boys of the world.

"It seems to be almost every man's complaint these days." She sat forward, the palms of her hands covering the backs of his, where they rested on the tablecloth. "You seem to be a dreamer, yet are a realist."

"I leave illusions to others." He decided that he really liked her.

A girl who wanted to be loved for herself always seemed to exclude her body from the inventory. Yet, when all was said and done, a girl's ecstasy areas were the only items worth having. Most often you could dispense with all of the rest.

He had no doubt that he would wake her up intellectually, and soon. But first she would have to be loved and roused to a furious passion. She would have to want and be wanted, correctly, for her body.

One day she would find out that he had lied to her —about where he lived and how he made his living. But now was not the time. She would find out soon enough, but not soon enough for her to cool down and change her mind.

She would find out about everything, but by then it would be too late. By then he would have sabotaged her into marriage, one way or the other. And she would be so sex-drunk that she'd do anything as long as there was a mattress beneath her and her beneath him.

He knew he would simply have to find somewhere, and soon. Four walls and a floor. But tasteful. One could hardly expect such a delicate plum to shed its blossom and be gobbled up by any sort of worm. One could not expect so much from such a nice, sensitive girl.

"I shall be perfectly honest with you, Aubrey. Your physiognomy does not exactly slay me. But you're very nice and for some reason you excite me. You're unmarried and not a nebbich. And you are respectable, confident and mature. Besides, you must be very clever and intellectual if you're a barrister. The money is of no account."

"Yes, of no account." But he was far away, dreaming about the crossroads where her legs joined. And there was such a lush forest that he just had to explore; in detail.

"Mind you, despite your physiognomy, you've got a very interesting face. Handsome in an unusual, unique way. Anyway, there's more to life than the mere physical."

"Yes." He almost swallowed the word. "More, much more." But so far he had only experienced that "more". Now he longed to experience the mere physical. She saw his disappointment and impulsively leaned forward, brushing his hand with her fantastic lips.

"I want to be loved for myself," she said.

He turned away, trying to assemble all the indifference he could muster, and looked at the silent couples at the other tables. All the girls would go home and say to mothers, "Guess why this night is different from all other nights?" And mothers, quick to remember that Passover was months away, would almost die inside as they replied, "Don't know, darling. Why is tonight so different? Been somewhere nice? Someone nice? What did you do? Dance? A show? Where did you go after?"

They'd soon show instant relief with hugs and kisses when all the Jewish daughters replied, "Met somebody fabulous tonight. But don't worry, Mummy. I didn't let him go too far."

No, Jewish mothers had no need to worry unless their daughters were in the hands of an Aubrey.

He looked around and around, and there was no doubt. What most girls had they would keep. Until some special Sunday when the mumbo-jumbo boys worked the magic to make the unmakable open their legs.

Even so, it was far too early to be sure about Zena, about the amount of money or persuasion he would need for his entrance fee. She was so unpredictable, so unblooded, and so far so much wanting to be wanted for herself.

She suddenly looked at her minute wristwatch. "Aubrey, I don't want to rush you, but we really must fly."

He complied, and they flew away in the Lotus Elan to Great Portland Street, where the Slightly Older Set were not aware that their way of life was about to be changed, forever.

11

The Wyckham Hotel, St. Marylebone—occasional venue of the Slightly Older Set when they were not rambling in the Chilterns or having deep and fascinating discussions on literature and life in each other's houses.

He took Zena's arm and descended the pile carpeted steps leading to the Derby Room. "The cream of Anglo-Jewry meet here." She spoke in hushed tones. "If a bomb dropped at this moment on this hotel, it would be a staggering loss for the Jewish community, and possibly for the rest of England. There's the committee."

In the foyer sat the hierarchy, who for democratic purposes called themselves the committee. But Aubrey wasn't fooled for one moment.

The secretary of the S.O.S. certainly was slightly older, but she still had a certain wistful sadness in her eyes when she smiled at him.

"Aubrey Field would like to become a member," Zena announced.

Aubrey smiled inscrutably while the committee studied him.

"Welcome," they said in unison.

"One guinea please," the treasurer quickly added.

"Pleased to have you with us." The President's

handshake was wet and limp and the tone of his voice pretentiously fruity.

"He's a barrister." Zena slowly mouthed the words to anyone who was interested.

"A barrister?"

"Oh, I don't think we have a barrister."

"No. We've got four accountants, one lawyer, three doctors, several businessmen, a few people in the shmutter game, a would-be-painter, four dentists, umpteen people who've been studying everything for ever, and now we have a barrister," said the podgy but quite desirable girl who was taking cash from the entrants.

Members were arriving all the time, and the foyer was becoming crammed with faces. Dreary faces, beaming faces, indifferent faces and just a few mad fiery faces.

"Do you always meet here?" he whispered into her ear.

"Oh no. Only for special occasions," Zena replied.

"What's so special about tonight? Everyone looks well dressed. Is the Prime Minister coming to address us?"

"Silly! We're having a charity dance."

"Dance! I can't dance." He would have turned round and left but the flow of people prevented this.

"Everyone can dance." Zena pouted a kiss towards him and hugged his arm.

"But—I'm not—dressed."

"First rule of the S.O.S.! We dispense with formality."

"But Zena, why didn't you tell me?"

"You wouldn't have come," she replied. "We have a fabulous band. Sebastian Marcus and his Silver Arrows! THE Sebastian Marcus. Don't look so worried, Aubrey. You don't have to dance. Very few people do."

He followed the multitude into the shimmering gold-gilt Derby Room, where soon the great minds of North-West London would come together because their bodies happened to need a fix of rhythm.

Aubrey noticed how everyone watched Zena's arrival. They simply could not help noticing her. She entered a room before she actually entered it, her breasts were advancing guards, reconnoitring for the rest of her.

The S.O.S. and their guests seemed to be a very fidgety lot as they lounged around the edge of the room, watching new arrivals and waiting for the band to stop tuning up and to start blowing, sucking, scraping and banging and thus give decent people an excuse to clutch other decent people indecently close.

"We should start at eight o'clock, but it's usually a Yiddisher eight o'clock," Zena whispered intimately, as if she were actually murmuring, "Ravish me tonight, Aubrey."

He didn't mind the delay. There was so much to study. Even lines of lined faces excited him; evoking dark and twisted dreams, dreams of fumblings in Finchley and moans coming from those little quiet streets of Willesden. And Aubrey could see in the half-light ageing nieces being stroked on stairs by a familiar face. "Uncle Ben! What you doing? Stop it! Stop! I'll die. I'll go mad. I'll scream," they all cried.

Aubrey laughed audibly at his most sordid imagination, then looked again at the male members of the S.O.S.

Many of them were going bald and were trying to look younger than their years. All in all, he felt rather sorry for these everlasting students. Indeed, some were actually wearing long university scarves around their necks, despite the stifling blast of central heating in the hall.

Aubrey sadly shook his head at these forgotten students who should have faced up to their lost youth long before the New Morality.

He wondered why he felt some disdain for most of the men, and he was worried that he might be judging them harshly. Not everyone had the courage and the capability to reject the past. Not every man was equipped to break out of the web of a mother's sticky love and follow his own star.

"I feel a sudden sense of purpose surging through me," he said.

"Oh Aubrey! You send me. I'm getting quite attached to you," Zena replied; whispering right into his ear. Her words were not unexpected, so he nodded. He wanted to analyse for her the complex reason why most males found it impossible to become men.

"Men are extinct Zena, and even women are dying out fast. We are utterly unique." He would have continued but at that precise moment Sebastian Marcus took up the baton and jerked his Silver Arrows into *Dig me Gravewise Lorelei*, which was the latest fabulous hit based upon a tuneful snatch of Wagner. The melody did not offend Aubrey, but he was rather astonished when he followed the dictate of his legs, and started pushing pulsing Zena around the hall.

12

"Well, did you like the crowd?" Zena sought his opinion.

"Some of them were rather nice," Aubrey replied, as they strolled towards the beautiful machine at the curb.

It was raining and the members of the S.O.S. were calling their goodbyes and zooming away in their cars. But some were walking towards the main road and Baker Street Station.

The President of the S.O.S. came out of the hotel and walked straight to Aubrey's car just as he squeezed beside Her Body.

"It's very nice you joining us. I'm very keen on having as many professional men as possible. I'm a professional man myself," Mr Moss said.

"Oh! Are you a doctor?"

"Actually—I'm an accountant." Mr Moss seemed to apologise.

Aubrey sent out one hand to clutch the unfortunate man on the shoulder. "I'm sure it must be very fascinating at times. What are you apart from that?"

The man seemed to shrivel as he shivered on the pavement. "I am very involved in the amateur dramatic world."

"Oh, you hanker after Hecuba."

"What do you think of Osborne?" the accountant asked.

"Not a bad little biscuit," Aubrey replied, and thought it a very suitable moment to leave, so he waved and shot away when the light changed to green, and he soon left them all behind.

"I love a car with chutzpah," he said.

He stopped in the park under a gathering of furious trees.

"I love Regents Park, but I don't know this part at all." There was a relentless quacking of an animal that she did not care for in the least.

"We're in the Inner Circle. Where children come in summer to feed the ducks and lovers come in winter to feed from each other."

He could see industrious young couples in practically every parked car.

When he kissed her eyebrows she raised them, because she obviously wasn't at all familiar with the nuances of love-making.

"I'm cold. I'm so very cold," Zena said. But she certainly was as warm as any radiator he had experienced, and although she didn't seem very happy, she did allow him to open the top button of her blouse and slip his hand on to her actual, beautiful, foamy flesh. "It's all right as long as it stays where it is," she said.

"Of course." He wanted to say more but he would have choked on words. Thoughts were safer so he thought and kissed her, and he could feel her straining to hold back the turbulent torrents of all her accumulated passion.

This time he would restrain himself, but next time he would force her to face the reality of the flesh. He would put his hand upon her knee and chant "Zena! Zena! Zena! Zena! Zena! Zena!" She would remove the hand, but he would put it there again,

[103]

and she would remove it once more. But he would persist and her resistance would slacken, bit by bit.

"I'll be perfectly honest with you Zena. Even I am only human. I cannot take you to my den because I could not trust myself within four walls alone with you," he would say.

But by then he would have her nipples. Black-berries ripe all the year round.

And Zena would be breathing heavily. "Oh Aubrey, you do things that make sense to me. I'm crumbling at your touch."

"Zena! I am burning for you and I have been honest with you. You worry me and I am afraid for you. Afraid because of the seas of passion that I know I can stir within you, for you are blessed with over-sexuality, I'm afraid. These oceans can drown us and that is why we must chart them thoroughly. Fortunately I am in control so therefore you must learn to trust me. Soon I will take you somewhere where I will un-dress you and show you exactly what to do. I will take you and take you."

"Aubrey darling, take me anywhere," she would moan.

But now their mouths were really meeting and a curious thing happened. She was not content to kiss him the way his aunt and his mother kissed him, the way he would have expected a respectable young lady to kiss. She was actually poking her tongue into his mouth. It was a nice tongue and he was sure that she did not have a contagious infection. It was just that it had taken him by surprise. And he didn't like it, it was no good pretending otherwise. Her tongue darting in and out of his mouth like a restless little lizard shocked him, but he did not want to hurt her feelings by stopping her.

It was utterly disgusting. He could not account for such behaviour from a respectable Jewish girl.

Yet is was wonderful. He also wanted to lizard her. It was disgustingly wonderful.

He drew his lips away. "God! We are insane. The engine's still running. Must stop it. I think we ought to go."

"Yes. We must, Aubrey," she sighed.

She was absolutely right. He was a hundred per cent in favour and echoed her sentiments. "I'm glad you're cooling down, Zena. You really are most over-sexed. A fault to the good. But you must be watched very closely. You need a man of experience." He started the car. "Shall we drive and never stop?" he said. "Let's drive all night straight into the dark."

Zena giggled and her grasp upon his shoulders loosened. Somehow he felt compelled to repeat what he had said. "Yes, I could drive you all night. Over and over again."

She looked sideways at him.

"I love driving. I really mean it. I'm a fanatic for eating up the tarmac," he added.

This seemed to reassure her and she stroked his shoulder again.

They remained silent for a while as the car shot towards St. John's Wood. "We must be patient Zena. We must never lose control." At that moment the car skidded to the other side of the road.

"Where you taking me Aubrey?" Zena looked concerned but she tried very hard to retain her over-emphatic smile.

He turned the car round and stopped.

"Isn't it odd? Instinctively I was driving towards Hendon. Like salmon, we Jews are programmed to move towards North-West London."

"Incidentally, where do *you* live?"

"Oh, didn't I tell you? Just round there in Avenue Road. The house is a trifle huge for my liking; you know Georgian houses. All right if you care for that sort of thing. Come then. On to Stamford Hill, to your waiting parents."

He was about to switch on the ignition, but she touched his hand. "Aubrey, darling, I'm not going straight home. Drop me here and get me a cab. You look tired."

"Nonsense." He did not need to hide his fury because he did not feel furious. In fact, he was delighted. He hated the Stamford Hill area, and avoided it whenever possible.

"I'll get out here." She already had the door open.

"I won't hear of it," he said, not only hearing of it, but getting out into the cold night air with her. "You won't be safe. Terrible scoundrels lurk everywhere." All he wanted to do now was to go home to bed, and get away from the howling wind. He hated trees when they self indulged this way.

"Aubrey darling! I've been around. Anyway, I've got to meet Daddy in the West End. He's there for a big Masonic do at the Connaught Rooms. He'll wait for me."

"I'll get you a taxi."

There were several cabs crawling along, and he hailed one. The driver was a Yiddisher boy with sexy eyes and bitten nails. He sported a most unseemly hairy chest through his unseasonal open-necked shirt.

Zena kissed Aubrey full on the mouth, and when he came back down to the pavement, the taxi was already speeding south to Zena's Masonic kosher butcher father.

Aubrey was about to drive home when he decided that the very least he could do was to inspect the road where he was supposed to be living. He entered Avenue Road where the houses were large and quite nice.

As he strolled he considered the various tales he had told Zena. And he did not feel in the least depressed.

[106]

Not having money was the only thing that prevented him from living here. After all, he could have been a barrister quite easily if Leah had had the foresight and unselfishness to allow him to study law. The scholarships would have been a walkover. And having become a barrister he would have easily soared to the peak of the profession and therefore he would have become fantastically wealthy and full of unbridled confidence. And with such confidence he would have persuaded his mother to leave Whitechapel for ever. And surely they would have settled in this very expansive and expensive road he was walking along.

It was all a natural sequence. The things he had told Zena would have been a logical culmination of events, had that natural sequence been allowed to start in the first place.

Fame, fortune and St. John's Wood were still his birthright, and they could still be achieved.

Aubrey stopped walking when he saw an overweight chauffeur peering closely at a grey Daimler with all the concentration of a butterfly-catcher. The man deftly flicked his podgy finger at a few minute but offending blemishes. He then started to polish the bodywork with a neurotic pride. Aubrey noticed that the car carried a diplomatic number-plate. But what sort of man was this to polish a Daimler by moonlight?

He approached, clutching the wad of fivers and tenners within his trouser pocket. Money communicated far better than Esperanto.

"Isn't she lovely? I go over and over her like this all day and every day," the chauffeur said, without turning around.

"Does she perform well?" Aubrey grinned at his distorted reflection upon the shining body.

"Performs fantastic. But only for me. But she demands a lot of care. Desires incredible amount of attention."

"Do you live here?" Aubrey asked.

"Here. Yes," the man replied. He panted breathlessly as he spoke, and stroked the gleaming surface lightly with his cloth.

"Maybe you can help me?" Aubrey said casually.

"If I cannot help you, my good sir, there would be no point in this conversation."

"I have a rather unusual request."

"Oh?" The chauffeur turned to face him. "I wish for you to be quite normal in what you desire."

"Of course. My dear fellow!" Aubrey wasn't quite sure what the man thought he might have had in mind, so he sounded just a little bit shocked. "I don't know what you're getting at."

"All right my friend, spit it out."

Aubrey noticed the huge open iron gate and the huge open garage which obviously housed the Daimler. He also noticed the detached white house which was as deep as it was wide.

"Yes; that's my boss's house. Cost a hundred thousand." The chauffeur puffed himself up another half an inch. "My boss is a diplomat. We are all diplomats," he added quietly, "Thank God. Now, what is your problem?"

"I need to borrow a room. In a large house."

"Don't we all? I have one myself, but don't we all?"

"I need a room for now and again. I'll be frank. A room for amatory purposes. A room to take someone to. To impress them." He took out the roll of notes and peeled four fivers from the main body. "I'm willing to pay."

"I love my boss. I worship him. How could I jeopardise my whole life's work?" He seemed sadly concerned.

"Are you a Yiddisher boy? You sound like one." Aubrey was surprised by the man's look of sudden wariness.

[108]

"A Yiddisher boy? Oh yes! I am a Yiddisher boy. We are all Yiddisher boys."

"Good. I'm sure you'll find a way if we can agree on a price."

"I could slip you in easy, any time. But how do I know you're not a spy? You might want to use a secret radio. Or lemon-juice and pigeons."

"My name is Aubrey Forbes-Levy and I live in Whitechapel and I am a respected and respectable Yiddisher Englishman."

The chauffeur shook Aubrey's hand vigorously. "Aubrey. Nice name. I'm trying to work things out. Because you're a Yiddisher boy, I'm searching my conscience. And even if you were a spy, at least you'd be spying for the right side."

"So it's yes?"

"Yes. I'll do it. Not for money mind you, but because one never knows when the situation will be reversed. We must all help each other."

"It's marvellous to meet someone so nice." Aubrey was about to put the four fivers back, but the chauffeur whisked them away with a magician's speed. But he had such a nice smile. You couldn't dislike such a man, no matter what he did. And of course he deserved the money. It was part of the deal.

"Fine. Twenty quid every time you need. First time you've already paid for. Every other time, you need only to pay half down, and other half when you've finished using interior sprung mattress." He stuck his finger into Aubrey's rib and laughed gaily.

"So, how do we fix it?" Aubrey hated to have to be practical, but he knew he was dealing with a man of the world.

The chauffeur led Aubrey along the gravel path, to the side of the house. "Don't worry, Aubrey," he whispered loudly. "See that door?"

Aubrey did. And he nodded.

[109]

"Call whenever you need to come. Give me few hours' notice if possible. I leave that door open. Any time you tinkle, day or night, it's open. Now that door opens into a passage that leads to one room only. This is your room. It's got bed and everything. You can tap away in that room to your heart's content. But take my advice, you never know. Bring a girl along with you just in case, just for cover. Then you can tap away all night to your heart's content." He winked, lit a yellow cigarette, and walked away to the back of the house, waving.

"Don't forget, keep in touch."

"What's your number. I say—what's your number?"

"Oh yes! My number is 999-4999. Just come when you need."

"And what's your name?"

"Ah yes—name? Ah yes. From one Yiddisher to another. I am Gregory Cohen. Never changed it. Take care." He disappeared into the dark.

"And mine's—Forbes-Levy," Aubrey shouted at no one. "Aubrey Forbes-Levy."

He left the drive and walked to where he had left the Lotus Elan. His temples throbbed and his heart was pounding. Everything was set and there was no turning back.

He jumped into the car and closed his eyes. There in the darkness he threw Zena upon the bed that took up practically the whole of that room. And there he undressed her. Slowly. She covered her eyes as he revealed her luminous, miraculous body. She was stark naked and openly panting for him. So he started her up and drove her madly fast, away, away from St. John's Wood and down, down, down towards the East End of London.

13

His car hurtled through the cardboard cut-out of the East End. It seemed like the full Jewish cast had been given the sack and had long ago departed.

And his father had departed; but alone, to avoid the exodus.

Aubrey drove his Elan into Hessel Street, but he remembered that such a car could be used as evidence against him, so he backed it out into the main road and parked it a few streets away.

It looked incongruous against the squat houses. Or maybe it was the street that was out of place. He sauntered towards his inevitable home, but fortunately he couldn't resist looking at himself in the window of the Palestinian Wine Shop. Somehow his reflection looked magnificent anywhere, since Zena. Then he received a tremendous shock. "Ye gods, I've got my Harrods on."

He rushed back to the car and from the boot he got the bundle of his father's clothing. It would never do for Queen Leah to know that he had spent some money that day on such excellent shmutter. He now had to transform himself back to assistant nebbich to the Queen of Sherbet.

He got back inside the car, unzipped, heaved off and threw aside the barrister gear, and changed back into the clothes that would leave his mother unastonished.

Two policemen were coming. His heart thumped with the excitement of it all. But he was sure that he was properly attired. There was no possible fear that his Zena stick would pop out and give them a raspberry.

He jumped out of the car just as the policemen drew level with him. People disappeared these days for far less than changing clothes in a Lotus Elan.

"Evening, Mr Feld. Sorry, I should have said Field. Been on a jaunt?" The older policeman winked and Aubrey tried to wink back, but he was not a very good winker. So he smiled. One always had to smile at the Law, even if they did get your name wrong. Those cups of tea and fags at the back of the shop certainly paid dividends in such back streets, where people weren't safe to wander abroad. "Be good, Mr Field."

Aubrey waved and walked on.

Not for one moment had he imagined they had approached him because of what circumstances had forced him to do at the bank. It was amazing; he was absolutely cool. The thumping of his heart and the sweat on his forehead were only to do with thoughts of original sin, and nothing worse.

He arrived outside the shop. It was shuttered, but there was a quiet sort of moaning coming from within: a low continuous sound from Leah and an intermittent descant from Auntie Beattie.

Why were they burning the midnight oil later than midnight in Hessel Street?

He knew he could easily slip inside and go to bed without them even noticing, especially the state they were in. So he opened the door with quiet precision and tiptoed over the threshold.

Leah and Auntie Beattie watched him is silence, like two stunned, red-eyed parrots who had lost their memories. Their moaning did not subside immediately, but continued for a while with automatic regularity, until it finally faded completely.

"Where have you been? What time you think it is? Where you been all day? If you're going to go—well, go. But let me know first."

"I have been out and I am going to bed."

"After all she did for you. Another mother like this there isn't in the world," Auntie Beattie said.

"I'm the best mother in the world," Leah said.

"You can say that again," Auntie Beattie said.

"Mother, I am changing my life. Now we shall see. Now we shall separate words from deeds."

But Leah wasn't listening. "I phoned the mortuary, the hospital, the police."

"Yes, in the order in which you wished to find me."

"I was the best mother in all the world. I ask no rewards. And if you found your feet at last, I hope they took you somewhere nice."

"You bet they did. I want to tell you something. Intimate."

"No!" They both covered their ears, but their eyes showed they were quite willing to lip read. "Don't Aubrey. Don't."

"You see, Mother, I have dirty thoughts."

"Oooh." Leah swooned rather badly into an uncomfortable position, so she pushed herself up and swooned all over again. "Oooh."

"You ought to know. I have tasted from the tree of life. I have hungrily gobbled up the delicious forbidden fruit. To be more precise, twenty-three times in the last year, mostly between 7.30 and 7.45 p.m., in Lisle Street, Soho. I am not pure. I have drunk from the tainted wonderful well of hell, almost every other Friday night, at five pounds a sin. And from now on I want it continuously. And for nothing!"

[113]

The sisters looked at each other like two visiting relatives at a looney-bin.

Aubrey turned towards his bedroom. "I love sex. S-E-X. I love it. I must have it. Now! Black, white or brown."

"Oh Aubrey! At least keep to nice respectable Jewish girls," Leah pleaded.

"Isn't passion divine? Auntie Beattie, when did you last have a wet dream?" He thought perhaps he was going a little too far, but if she understood what he said, it served her right for having such a dirty mind. And if she didn't understand, then he was acting well within the bounds of decency.

"Oh, help! Save me. Hear what he said? Leah, I mustn't hear." She understood. It was absolutely disgusting.

He grabbed his aunt close. "What do you want? The milkman? Yummy! Lots of double cream. Or the baker? Beattie darling, try my lovely hot Vienna roll. Or the butcher? Hello, Beattie, have I got a nice bit of meat for you!"

Leah went to the phone, lifted it, waited. Then she realised she had forgotten to dial, so she replaced the receiver. "I just want you to know I almost phoned the emergency strait-jacket people," she said to her mad son. Then she turned to comfort her sister, but this proved impossible, for Beattie was standing on a chest of drawers, sobbing pitifully, but without tears.

"Come down! Come down! Beattie! Come down. Or they'll think it's in the family," Leah hissed angrily. "What you doing up there?"

Beattie gave an apologetic smile and started to descend, slowly and without one extra hand to assist her.

"I just want you to know that I want what every man wants, above and below the waist, from every woman between sixteen and twenty-nine." Now it was done. Now she would release him and he would be free of her, and therefore need to take no other measures.

He sat down to read again the five-year-old copy of House and Garden.

"Shall I make you a nice cup of tea?" Auntie Beattie beamed as if nothing had happened. And soon she was humming and clattering about in the kitchen.

"Aubrey, Aubrey, I feel you're slipping away from me." Leah tugged his lapels. "You're slipping, Aubrey, you're slipping away. I don't know you any more. I'm glad you may be going away, but I don't want you slipping."

Through his half closed eyes he smiled at her. For once in her life she was right. He sighed to himself. "Oh Aubrey. You're fagged out. You think too hard." Not waiting for tea he left them there.

Upstairs he went, yawning and yawning. And he felt marvellous.

He did not undress, in case he decided in the middle of the night to leave just like that. So he only took his shoes off before slipping into bed.

Soon he was dreaming of his glorious father who was throwing gold sovereigns from the receding dark. They were pelting down upon him. The whole universe was pouring with gold, and Father, with his whirring helicopter moustache, smiled down, his face filling the whole sky. But far away Aubrey hoped he hadn't offended Auntie Beattie by not having her cup of tea.

14

Dawn haggled with Hessel Street and finally decided to buy a bit of space.

Aubrey looked out of his window and watched for the approach of morning. And there it was, nothing could stop it now. So he just waited whilst dawn brought more and more and more of the street into the world.

The day of the Asian had returned to Hessel Street with the usual yodelling from Radio Karachi seeping through the wall that separated his bedroom from Mr and Mrs Ibrahim's.

One hundred years of hungry bugs had nearly eaten away the walls. They were only kept upright by the wallpaper on either side.

The usual curry smell arrived with full light. It covered this entire world where once the sublime essence of chopped liver reigned supreme.

Aubrey thought of his boyhood as he slowly put on his shoes.

In his adolescence he had gone slightly off the rails. No one would believe that now, but it was quite true. In those days he believed in good, evil, peace, respect and even God. And tranquility. In those days he even intoned a prayer that belonged to no particular sect: "Peace is above me, around me, within me, about me. I am peace. I live in peace."

This morning he prayed again: "Curry is around me. Curry is within me, and curry is about me. I am curry. I live in curry. I am a curry-basher." He intoned this as he walked downstairs towards the street door.

"Aubrey! Where you going? Aubrey!" Her face turned institution-green as she stood clutching at her frail body. "Where you going Aubrey?"

"Out!"

"Out? Where? This time of day? Why do I have such aggravation? Maybe you need a sea cruise, by yourself."

"I'm going for a ramble into the country."

"Which country? Israel. I've got your passport somewhere." She was already looking around, trying to remember where she had put it.

"I am going for a walk into the English countryside. For fresh air and birdsong." He enunciated each word, perfectly.

"Fresh air will kill you. And then what bird will marry you?" She came over to him. "Aubrey. Tell me. What's troubling you? I'm your only friend in this world, which is the only one, I hope."

"I am drifting away from you. In mind and body. You're not only losing a loving son, Mother, you're gaining loneliness." He hated being cruel, but he knew what he was doing. If she hated him enough, it would help her over the long days of her never-ending years ahead.

"I'll make bread pudding before you go. Take it with you. Bread pudding goes down nice on rambles."

"It's time you knew, Mother, that I hate your cooking. Especially your bread puddings."

"I wish I was dead. I wish I was back in Russia, which amounts to the same thing," she cried. "What would you do then?"

[117]

"I'll survive without you," he shouted back.

"Good. I'd like to see you survive, if you don't kill yourself."

He hurried out of the house and rushed along the street determined that this time he would never return.

But when he turned the corner he felt unusually cold, so he performed a smart about-turn and walked back towards his home.

There was plenty of time for the ramble. The Slightly Older Set were still turning over in their beds and dribbling upon their pillows, refusing to admit another day was about to make them even more older and set and even less slightly.

He approached the shop with confidence. Leah most likely had returned to her bed, especially after her performance of a few minutes before.

And sure enough, when he re-entered the house he found everything quiet. Leah was nowhere to be seen, but he knew this tranquillity could not last.

She would emerge soon with her camphor-impregnated presence. She would materialise from where she now was, licking her wounds and bottling her tears. And, Auntie Beattie would appear at any moment, with flushed face and heartburn, looking as usual as if she had heard about the cataclysm on the eight o'clock news. But he didn't mind.

He had a little time to kill, and death was always kinder and easier to bear when you shared it with loved ones.

Sometimes he secretly welcomed returning to the family fold, even if it was only for a few moments, for he seldom got the opportunity to hear talk about himself. Once he had heard that listeners never hear good of themselves. This was probably true but it would not deter him. He very much wanted to hear her villifying him. It would make no difference to his impending departure. Indeed, it would help.

[118]

But there was another motive for eavesdropping; he loved hiding in the dark. All through his childhood he had enjoyed hearing her become frantic in case he had had an accident and was dead forever. He wanted to see his mother's real grief, her genuine devastation for his seemingly untimely departure.

He wanted to assess how well she would be able to cope in the Aubreyless years ahead. It would have given him much comfort to know that she would only lose control of herself and fall down unconscious. He could not bear to think of her slashing her neck and wrists with the highly-sharpened rarely used best carving knife. Not that anything she did to herself could deter him any longer from leaving her alone from this morning on.

So he crept into the darkness of the old wardrobe and smothered himself with the discarded clothing of his childhood. But his hand found a dusty wine bottle in a corner. He removed the cork, and breathed in the heady smell of antique cherries. His mother must have made the stuff years ago.

He quickly replaced the cork and thrust the bottle into his trouser pocket. It was said that a new ice age was on its way. One had to be prepared for all eventualities.

He could hear Auntie Beattie singing in the shop. "It's only a shanty in old shanty town."

Then he heard the unmistakable vinegar voice of his mother.

"Hello, hello. That the Fineberg Detective Shop? Hello, hello!"

Beattie was serving now, continuing her song probably with a lump of her favourite stick-jaw in her mouth. The till was ringing continuously.

"I wish to report the loss of my son. I don't mean his disappearance. No. I mean his strange manners. Hello, hello. Am I talking to Fineberg? Hello? Is that the Fineberg Detective Corporation? Put me through to your president. Oh, listen, I want for you to work for me. For cash. How much you charge?"

"Givme. Givme."

"No, Beattie. Leave it alone."

They were obviously struggling for the instrument. Auntie Beattie had a bee in her bonnet that she was good on phones. This time she won the battle for the mouthpiece. "It's a very personal matter. My sister, Mrs Leah Feld, is minus a lot of money. We're not saying. But if you must know, from the sum she's got in her bank. Embezzled she was. From her banking account."

The words struck like lightning.

Aubrey crouched down in the dark and waited, and he wondered how they could have discovered so soon.

But it was not the thought of prison that caused an icy coagulation of blood within his veins. There was also another reason for the feeling that his heart was going under for the third time.

It was true that captivity carried certain compensations of escape, security and even respect, but the loss of unscrewed Zena carried nothing except a prison mattress with more holes than the moon's surface. Before the dark mists of Dartmoor he just had to know Zena, in the Biblical sense.

How could he be expected to rot happily without her having once opened her thighs, so that he could conjure up incredible memories for all those thousands of nights ahead? For only regular hand-drill could possibly keep him in touch with the rest of mankind.

"Hello! Is this the Fineberg Detective Agency? Hello! Hello!"

He crawled out of the wardrobe on all fours, past where they were sighing and crying in unison; and they did not notice him stand upright, nor did they notice his hands imperceptibly inching up the stippled woodwork and gently pushing the door open.

The day eagerly poured through the crack as if it was fleeing from the streets. Soon he would be away. Soon, soon. And his one Achilles' heel, his non-conformist tummy, could just about make it.

The bell pinged.

"Damn my fat stinking belly. It's got a mind of its own," Aubrey shouted as he scuttled into the street, into a crowd of bantering, bartering Asians, where he reduced his offending bulge by making himself as tall as possible.

A Hebrew needed height. A Hebrew was as tall as any Moslem, any day of the week, especially on the Christian Sabbath. Taller! Hebrews were giants and could take giant strides. So he took Hessel Street in one or two Chagall leaps, as he dwelt calmly upon the latest turn of events.

There was not a man in or above the world who could apprehend Aubrey Field. Yet Mr Fineberg nagged at him. That name somehow evoked a man of exceptional ability.

But, when he could see the end of Commercial Road, he became certain of one thing. He did not care one fig for the Fineberg Detective Syndicate. "Let them send their best man. Let them send a minyan of Private Eyes."

He found himself moving into the increasing number of Sunday sleep-walkers who poured in from the suburbs and were now converging towards the spider's web of Petticoat Lane.

Aubrey decided to walk the other way, towards the river, where swans would not be rummaging for substandard pieces of formica or shagged-out strips of neon tubing.

The river flowed as usual, but here nothing else moved

except the clouds scooting across the sky from west to east.

Each cloud was a dead relative. They yawned, laughed, waved and turned their backs, then they lined up like greyhounds before racing across the sky to some winning post the other end of France.

The wind howled through silent wharves. The wind was also a blackleg. "Can you loan me half a crown, Mrs Goldberg? Can you loan me a pound of potatoes, till Friday, Mrs Goldberg?"

"Why don't you assimilate, bloody Jewish wind, or go to Israel?" Aubrey shouted at his cantering, disappearing, grey uncles.

"Too late for Zion," the wind cried. "Too late for Zion. We pawned our harps and lost the ticket."

The tugs on the river burped. "Oy, Mrs Smulevitch, have I got heartburn. Rachmunis, Mrs Goldberg, you need rachmunis."

'Rachmunis! Rachmunis! For why should I need rachmunis, Sarah Smulevitch? I need rachmunis for myself," Mrs Goldberg howled back.

"Shut up the both of you. I need rachmunis. I need compassion for myself," Aubrey yelled.

Silence was the reply. Boats, not being people, sometimes did not feel the need to answer.

There was absolutely no one about. Except a solitary seagull slowly circling a patch of tar. And there were no more sounds; just the Thames slapping the stones beneath him.

The same river had delivered his mother and father from the belly of Russia when all the Jews had come pouring in and pouring in. But most of those were now minus eyeballs.

If only he had the patience and respect to give her a real send-off. If only he could send her back to where she came from. Surely Russia was vast enough to contain even Leah? If only he could have spared the time to shove his beloved mother back to Odessa, where she claimed that she was born.

Aubrey loved the Thames because it was so unchanging. People had to develop, that was the role expected of them, but the Thames was exempt from criticism. It was too old to change anyway. And whatever you thought or dreamed one fact was indisputable. The Thames was the most truly splendid Jewish river in the world, by adoption, and that included the Hudson and the Jordan.

He decided to toast the river with his mother's vintage cherry brandy. "Lochaim! Please God by you! You wet Jewish bastard. I wish you'd take my mother back. Be a sport. We Jews must help each other."

But he felt suddenly bored with the river. All it could do was creep along between here, there and nowhere. So Aubrey walked away, backwards, waving gaily at the whole empty panorama surrounding him, just in case he was being observed by a dangerous sexual maniac who easily could have been watching him from the other side of the river, with a telescope or opera-glasses, pinched from the Royal Opera House, Covent Garden.

He was glad to see the back of the ominous water, and whistled as he merged with the converging Sunday people. From Hanwell and Watford and Hornsey the grey mass came because they simply could not exist one day longer without five square yards of formica and a plastic tea-set.

Aubrey sauntered past smoked salmon slicers, body-builders, weight-guessers, curers of corns and nervous systems. He stood for a moment by the tipsters and wondered why these men should share such rare knowledge with Middlesex somnambulists. Surely if these hoarse gurus had the answer and did not bother to apply it to themselves, they could at least make a few bob more in a nicer postal district?

Soon he left all the crowds behind and strolled alone through deserted streets. He wasn't sure whether it was late, because his watch had stopped in the cemetery, days before. He was always prone to overwind watches at burial grounds.

The shops and stalls of Spitalfields market were closed. It was like an area evacuated before an impending disaster.

In Spital Square the smell of sweet rotting oranges penetrated everywhere. In these very streets Jack the Ripper roamed, and not so very long ago. Possibly this particular smell of rotting fruit had caused Jack to rip so many fallen women so that they could never stand upright again. The impotent sun cast his long shadow along the ground. It seemed to stretch and stretch further than his tired legs cared to go.

So he sat upon a broken orange box and watched the few lonely pigeons strutting around. One cooed so monstrously as it stared at him with its raving red eyes, he was sure it was Anti-Semitic.

Aubrey stared back because he was not afraid even if the bird was a small but deadly falcon in disguise. Any moment now it would probably start going for his lips, eyeballs and genitals.

"Just you try," Aubrey growled, pulling a Japanese war face, and continuing with some rather excellent cat impersonations.

The hawk with its few decoy friends flew off and Aubrey felt wonderfully happy. He took out the bottle of wine to celebrate the fact that he had not been disfigured, and when he swigged the delicious fluid, it radiated right through him, bringing more and more sunshine to the day.

But soon the bottle was empty. "That's odd! I never drink. Wonder where it all went?"

There was the possibility that he might conceivably have finished the cherry brandy all by himself, but this idea was so extraordinary that he dismissed it and decided to forget about the cherry brandy altogether.

But Aubrey suddenly thought he could see Leah and his heart missed a beat.

Her face was now hidden by the wheel of a market barrow, but he was certain Leah was there, stalking him with all the righteousness of a thwarted mother.

He searched for a phone-box that actually worked, but Leah's shit-brown shadow fell across the entire road.

He then sprinted towards Liverpool Street Station, but his way soon became blocked by a giant apparition that was causing a traffic jam. People stood around laughing and pointing as the thing ate every bowler hat in sight. He wondered why on earth his mother had acquired a voracious appetite for such an incredible item of apparel.

Aubrey was certain that this was not a dream. Dreams were always about rather fantastic yet ordinary things, like Matterhorns or waterfalls or dismembered torsos. Having decided that it wasn't a dream, he felt no need to pinch himself. But there she was sitting on top of the railway station and then scuttering around deserted platforms, on all eights.

"My Yiddisher momma, I miss her more than ever now," he crooned very beautifully, just like Sophie Tucker.

Leah came towards him and sniffed him loudly with nostrils as huge as Rotherhithe tunnel.

"What do you want, Mother?"

"I want for you to be happy. Let me eat you. You won't have to worry no more."

"I threw my mother in the air. She fell to earth in Spital Square," he said, tossing the monster as he glided eastward.

But he never seemed able to lose Leah. Her shadow never failed to catch up with him.

"What must I do to escape?" he pleaded.

"You were tempted, Aubrey. When you're not tempted, you're happy."

He picked up a grapefruit from a clean piece of pavement. It was not altogether rotten and he found a few sucks left in it, chucked it away down the empty pitch, heard applause from two million bones and football chanting from a million skulls. But he wasn't unduly put out. "Any applause is better than none."

Uncertainties belonged to lesser men. Leah scurried alongside, brushing the pavement with her eight hairy legs. The borough council would have paid handsomely for her services.

She swept a path towards his chilblains. And he was in such agony that he did not feel ashamed to take out his proud pink prodder and urinate steamy golden rain over each single toe.

Leah now loomed higher than all the tenements of the neighbourhood, and soon shops and motor-cars had to put on their lights.

He wanted to get away, but her tentacles guarded every road.

"Trust me, Mother. You must trust me."

"I trust everyone, when they're dead. I'll trust you. Soon."

"Go back to your box of bananas," he replied, sitting on the pavement, weeping and picking his toenails. "I always trusted you," he sobbed without much conviction, "Until my middle leg problems got in the way. Why's it so dark? Where's the sun gone?"

"Since when did the sun have to consult me? Enjoy Aubrey, while there's time. Pretend people are monkeys, then people won't upset you. Don't look so worried, Aubrey. Your brows are knitted."

[126]

"In what colour?"

"Stop joking and listen. Aubrey, this is the age of beasts. People are either monkeys, worms, ants or snakes. Nothing else exists."

"Where can I hide?" He tugged one of her legs, and it came right away in his hands, but did not bleed excessively.

"Mother, I must start living soon. I want to arrive."

"Arrive? Arrive? Who arrives? In the cemetery you'll arrive. Enjoy yourself. Dance before your legs turn to water."

Aubrey mazurka'd past the kosher slaughterhouse, partnering the severed leg of his mother. "What shall I do with this?"

"Do what you like, I've got plenty more," Leah the spider replied before slithering upon the sea of lethal lullabies; a sea that she was spinning as she sailed upon the never-ending stickiness of existence.

He danced and danced the other way, away from her to where a church clock was striking the eleventh hour.

He could have scooped off his sweat and filled a tumbler with it, if he had had such a strange inclination.

"Fly! You are undone," Leah called from far away.

Aubrey zipped himself decent and remembered that he had a rendezvous in thirty minutes. So he gladly left the cold wet world for the busy warmth of Liverpool Street Station.

Leah was nowhere to be seen; but her voice still persisted in the steam of the trains. "Fly! Fly! Fly without wings. Try to get away from the web where you are warm."

Aubrey went down beneath the platforms. And there, in the underground, he caught a Circle Line train to Baker Street, the S.O.S., and Zena.

15

He held the scrawny neck beneath the stinking green surface. She looked up at him like a cockatoo pathetically trying to squawk its last. But he did not relent and held her wriggling bones under the slimy water.

Bubbles of air came from her nostrils and popped on the surface.

Aubrey couldn't be absolutely certain, but she looked like his own mother. He wondered why he was drowning her so happily.

He knew he was happy because he could see his joy reflected in the patches of unpolluted lake.

This appalled him. For there was absolutely no logical reason for him to slowly quench his only mother so permanently. Yet he was doing just this with a deep feeling of pleasure.

But he was even more pleased that all this was a dream he was dreaming on a train which was returning to London from the tyranny of brickless meadows.

And he was quite aware that Zena was blowing on his face. So he woke up.

"Why did you wake me? I was having such a lovely —" He stopped himself, closed his eyes, and bit into the peppermint that he offered himself. "I was having a terrible nightmare. Thanks for waking me."

Aubrey looked around the train, and then out of

the train. The fields of Buckinghamshire slipped past with considerable speed. It was wonderful to return to the city where the sky did not watch you all the time like a peeping Tom.

People didn't realise how lucky they were that all the green stuff would soon be gone, forever.

He had tried hard in the past to see just what sentimentalists meant when they pointed rapturously at fields of ordinary wheat. But he had failed to experience the excitement.

No one could accuse him of intolerance, and he readily accepted that it took all sorts of stupid bastards to make a world. They were all entitled to their own opinions, even if ninety-nine per cent of them should have been forcibly locked away.

"Why you screwing up your face?" Zena asked, her private central-plant going full blast and scorching his very flesh through his very thick clothing. "Are you feeling all right?"

"It's the countryside, Zena. I have never approved of it to be honest. I've never been over-impressed by all that unbuilt-on wasteland."

"Don't you find nature fascinating?"

"Nature is all very well, if you like that sort of thing. But I believe it's rather overdone."

The members of the Slightly Older Set who shared the compartment gawped at him nervously, but with respect.

"I have never been consumed by a passionate desire for grass." All his new acolytes watched his every expression and grimace with intent, listened to each word with adulation. They were moths, needing a new flame in their darkness, getting a moment's glow for their fragile wings before they crumpled so soon into dust.

But Aubrey did not feel sad for soon he would re-enter the concrete paradise of St. Marylebone.

[129]

"Did you enjoy the ramble?" Zena hoped, but she wasn't sure.

Aubrey smiled. He could afford to be kind. Baker Street would be looming in no time at all, and the ordeal would be as dead as Golders Green on Yom Kippur.

"What can one say about rambling? You go from nowhere to nowhere for no reason. It was a ramble."

Aubrey watched the other members of the S.O.S. as they pushed into the already crammed compartment. People never ceased to amaze him, they were so un-amazing, so typical of themselves.

Didn't the sufferers from acolytis know there was no cure for self-immolation? But then, possibly one burning moment of truth was worth a whole lifetime of drab uniformity.

Zena touched his hand as he stared out of the window at the dark flashing landscape.

"A penny for them." She waved, bringing him back from the universe.

He turned to her. Only Zena deserved his attention; she alone had the depth and capacity to be stirred and be made larger by his own overwhelming desire to stir her and make her larger.

"All right then, twopence," she added.

"I was actually thinking, pity the S.O.S. waste such priceless time on rambles."

"Do you think so? We're all going to Cookham next Sunday."

"I hope not. I had thought my rambling days were over, Zena. I do not see the point in it," he intoned on one note, not unlike a rabbi reading a portion of the Law.

"What would you suggest instead of rambling?" she said, without the slightest suggestion of a sneer.

He sensed that she was waiting for a bombshell.

"I always had this compulsion to change things. To

shake up everyone I meet, to shatter long held illusions."
He wondered what the hell he was saying. Then he
stopped wondering as she held his hand and squeezed it.
He longed and longed to play a game of squash with her.
"Oh, there's so much to do—if only there were time.
But I'm so involved."

"What would—you: I mean, what changes would
you make if you were president of the S.O.S.?"

"President? Me, president?"

"Why not? Why not you?"

"Darling girl. I simply had not thought of such a
thing. The real trouble is that those with real genius
are far too busy, so that an important body like the
S.O.S., I'm sorry to say, have second-raters to run it. But
of course the very very best sort of second-raters."

"Aubrey—I know it's a lot to ask, but why don't you
consider considering the presidency."

He continued to study his face in the window of the
train. "There's so much to do. I can think endlessly
of so many marvellously exciting acts."

"You seriously must consider leading us, Aubrey,"
she whispered.

"I had intended orifice—" He quickly corrected the
ridiculous slip of the tongue, "I did intend office over
some august body, one day. Who knows? Perhaps I
will take over the S.O.S. and put us on the map."

Outside, the train was grinding to a halt and all
the others were getting impatient, but Zena could not
take her eyes from his.

"Aubrey! How different you are. How original and
exciting you make life become."

He could almost have stayed beside the dark Buckinghamshire fields for ever, but the train shunted forward
reluctantly towards the outer suburbs of London, and
he was not displeased. One of the boys played plaintively
upon a harmonica. He wore such an obvious toupee to

cover his foredome that it was not surprising that he looked deeply sad.

"Yes. Maybe I will become President of this great society. There would be a new voice to contend with in Anglo-Jewry, and we will be a light unto the rest of our community. In the beginning, we shall shine forth upon these clouded hills but later be a spectre to haunt Europe and far beyond the sceptred isle, until we affect this entire earth of majesty."

Aubrey often wondered where his words came from. This inner language sometimes took over and then there was nothing to do but follow its authentic voice. Once uttered, the words brought about the reality they prophesied.

"Zena, I think I shall take over." His voice was emotionless, firm but kind.

"Aubrey, you're dynamite."

"Yes."

"Please be kind to me," she whispered.

"I'll try. But you must trust me implicitly."

The train had now stopped again and the giggling of the girls had given way to a sing-song.

It was obvious that they were resigned to accept whatever fate had in store for them, realising they had nothing much to lose except the one precious commodity they were extremely unlikely to lose under these circumstances. But he loved them all, without exception, as they sang in unison. After all they were his golden fleece. So he sat back to enjoy the old songs of the Slightly Older Set.

"Solomon and David lived immoral lives,
They went around flirting with other people's wives.
In the end their consciences began to give them qualms,
So Solomon wrote the Proverbs and David wrote the Psalms."

Aubrey wondered how these people would react when he brought fame to them. He would bring them to the notice of the world by placing them incessantly upon the front pages of the Jewish Chronicle. The name of the society would soon become a household word and they would be discussed, vilified and lionised whenever and wherever the passions of Anglo-Jewry became aroused. If they had but known their fate, they would have all got out of the train and pushed it happily by hand, all the way to Baker Street.

He decided to sing along with them; after all, a President Elect was also a member of the society. He knew the ribald words but did not know how he knew them. And he certainly knew the swelling melody.

It was "Deutschland Uber Alles", which, on the face of it was a surprising choice for an Anglo-Jewish organisation. But the words seemed appropriate enough:
"Life presents a dismal picture,
   Dark and gloomy as the tomb.
   Father's got an anal stricture,
   Mother's got a fallen womb.
   Sister Sadie's been aborted
   For the twenty-seventh time;
   Brother Harry's been deported
   For a homosexual crime.
   Amen!"

The train reached Baker Street after only a fifty-minute delay. Aubrey got off and went straight to a top station official. He had long since discovered the futility of complaining to the lower echelons.

The official had meat strands between his teeth, but he was courteous and explained the exact reason for the delay. Aubrey approved of such a rare display of honesty and he thanked the man. Then he went back to the shivering congregation.

"I have had words with the top man here. He assures me that the delay was not caused by cussedness at all. There's a far more understandable reason. Apparently the lines are being modernised so that trains of the future will literally be able to fly to and from this metropolis. Therefore we must expect slight hold-ups."

They seemed satisfied and grateful, and went shuffling happily back to the security of their furnished box of bricks that kept out briar and bramble.

He and Zena watched the last S.O.S. disappear. Then without a word he took her arm and they glided into the sanctity of the fume-ridden streets.

Zena stood and breathed in a little of the poison, throwing her mauve scarf around her face, leaving just her endless eyes uncovered. These were to watch him with unswerving adoration all the way through the concrete jungle of St. Marylebone.

Earlier there had been a slight fog, and even though he could still smell the final traces hanging on the air there was not one solitary wisp of it to be seen. Miraculously, like the Red Sea, it had vanished before them.

"And my name isn't even Moses," Aubrey spoke. She did not quite understand, yet in a purely instinctive sense she caught on.

"It could be. If you can take command of the S.O.S. and make them follow you, nothing is impossible.'"

She almost hung upon his arm as he led her to the car and entered with her into the secure-smelling interior.

Again they went silent. Zena seemed to sense that he had made up his mind to do something very special tonight. She was a wise girl and knew that sometimes words were entirely unnecessary. Zena knew the score. She understood that there came a time in one's life when one had to fight against the barricades of one's own self and blindly follow one's instinct. They were certainly on the same wavelength. And he hoped the frequency would be strong and often.

"So we'll go straight to your place." Aubrey's heart thumped as he uttered the words.

"Yes," she replied. "It's got to happen sooner or later."

"No matter what anyone thinks. It just has to be this way. Direct."

Usually there was no short cut to the bedroom of a Jewish girl; one simply had to go straight through the living-room of her parents, and be introduced to them. For only the Jewish mother and father possessed the combination that unlocked the legs of every Jewish girl; except Zena.

Silence descended again. But he sat back, looked up at the heavens and relished the moment. He had never seen such a sky.

"Do you mind this moment of reverie?" He did not look at her and though she did not reply he knew she was sitting upon a fiery furnace which, once opened, would lick away the world with insatiable tongues of flame. Zena could be satisfied by few men upon this earth.

He lightly kissed her nostrils and he could feel both her titties gushing coloured sparks which whizzed away up into the sky. And her belly button gushed fountains of fire from never-ending catherine wheels, whilst his own beautiful prick was an enormous rocket which one normally reserved to climax an incredible firework display.

The fuse was already lit and it stood up proudly, ready for the universe, until it fizzed and fizzed and shot hot sparks back at its launching post, and it was all set to break away. And then it shot towards a milky way that it miraculously was providing for itself.

Aubrey never quite returned to earth, but nevertheless, trivial earth things niggled. It wasn't the dampness rusting his trouser zip that worried him, but how he would explain away to Leah the starchy patch on his underpants. But tonight he zoomed high over Baker Street, looping the loop over the Planetarium until all the dead of London awoke and pointed up at him. Then he cascaded back to the pavement, to her.

"You were quite incoherent on the ramble. I was worried."

"Oh?" He didn't quite know how to reply.

"You stumbled umpteen times and said such funny things."

"Yes. I am only truly myself on solid pavements. The countryside upsets me, and there is also you. You have had such an effect upon me it's a miracle I have sounded as logical as I have."

This seemed to please her and she squeezed his hand.

Thus electrified, he turned the ignition key once and despite the extreme coldness which had gripped the entire day, the engine purred obediently, and he drove towards Stamford Hill.

For the entire journey neither of them uttered one sound except for the deep urgent breathing which added excitement to the fast but extremely unreal journey over the crust of the singing undulating streets.

But before Aubrey had even thought about what he would do next, Stamford Hill in all its mad, mad, exciting urban splendour loomed up before them.

He stopped the car near a cluster of voluble chassidim who still wore clothes of mediaeval Poland and had never heard of Einstein, Epstein or Gertrude Stein, even if they were all part of that same race who had chosen God. Their long side curls seemed quite fashionable.

Not too far along the road Aubrey noticed the ever-waiting air-raid siren. If it blew at this moment he and Zena still had four minutes to pass the time. And

Aubrey was sure that even a Jewish girl would hardly prevaricate under those circumstances.

Her warm fingers slid along his hand. Each finger had a life of its own, gently exploring the almost audible flesh of his knuckles, palm, wrist and forearm.

"Aubrey—I'm thrilled you intend to take what is truly yours."

She said it so beautifully. It was as if she were asking him to accept a creamy, crumbly meringue that she was offering through see-throughable gossamer wrapping.

"When shall—" he swallowed the spit of excitement, "When can I do it, Zena?"

"Don't ask me. Go ahead as soon as you like."

"I couldn't do it without you really wanting me to."

"I do. I do. I can't wait now."

Aubrey was glad she came straight out with it. He despised people who indulged in double meaning. A single meaning was difficult enough to navigate through to another person's understanding. Yet when he was with Zena all doubts drifted and vanished and he knew exactly what he had to do.

"Is it possible your parents may not approve?" he shot to her out of the blue serge night.

"Why shouldn't they?"

He laughed. Sometimes he was capable of saying the most ridiculous things. Who were her parents to approve or disapprove? If she could do better than a top barrister who was neither married not perverted it was up to them to uncover him. They could certainly rest on their laurels so far.

Aubrey noticed Zena's finger pointing directly towards the butcher shop.

"That your place? Oh yes! Kosher Butcher."

"There are many worse ways of earning a living."

"Please, Zena, I beg you. Do not apologise. There's nothing to be ashamed of. As long as he likes me and doesn't get struck off for selling non-kosher flesh."

"MORRIS CONWAY—KOSHER BUTCHERS OF QUALITY." The ill-designed sign said in peeling, fading gold.

Aubrey was glad. At first he had imagined that Mr Conway was rolling in money. He had never doubted that Zena's father owned a string of kosher butcher shops. Aubrey had to admit he had given himself this impression. Zena had never suggested that her people were anything other than little people with a little money. But he was glad. There was always the greater thrill of scooping someone right out of the soulless existence of a shop. Zena would truly relish freedom.

Aubrey chuckled fearsomely, like one waking from a nightmare only to find that doomsday has arrived.

"Oh, it must be fun, living in Stamford Hill," he said, getting out of the car and opening the door for her.

"It's not bad. Plenty of worse places," Zena replied, revealing the best places of all; the tops of her thighs, as she climbed out into her world.

"I can hardly wait to be with you—to see the inside of your—of your dwelling place." He closed his eyes and clutched his forehead.

"You alright?" Zena asked as she walked ahead towards the door.

Aubrey nodded. He wasn't quite sure whether it was the sight of her flesh or the after-effects of the cherry-brandy which caused his head and Stamford Hill to spin. But he braced himself for the inevitable moment, for the baptism of fire. Nausea or not, he could not fail her.

"I'm so happy, Aubrey, at last it's all happening. I can't wait. I'm so happy." She tried to push the Yale key into the lock and seemed surprised that it didn't work. "Oh, I can't get it in."

"Let me put it in for you." He smiled blandly, inserted the key the wrong way up and pushed it straight home. "After you," he said, gently pushing the door open.

Zena entered and Aubrey followed her into the corridor. He was glad to get away from the street because the noise inside his head was quite excruciating.

But there was also blatant sound from the bowels of the house. It was obviously coming from a television set. Then he noticed a lighted room at the other end of the corridor. He and Zena were obviously not alone.

"Are—your parents home?"

She looked surprised. "Of course. Where should they be? You did want to meet them, didn't you?"

"Yes! Yes! Of course I do. I just thought we might have been deprived of their company."

"I'm so pleased we're all coming together at last." Zena took off her coat and walked towards the torture chamber. "I hope you're not disappointed."

"Disappointed? Me? Why should I be? What could we do here by ourselves to pass the time anyway?"

He could see she didn't quite understand the connection between her statement and his reply, but she had the good grace to continue smiling as she opened the door of the living-room.

Aubrey followed her and smiled with even greater grace, considering his head was about to burst.

16

The woman glanced up from her fat paperback, and the man from the fat chicken he was plucking.

"Hello," the woman said.

"Hello," the man said.

"Hello," Zena said. "This is Aubrey."

"Hello," Aubrey said, shaking hands with the woman.

"Hello, Aubrey," the man said.

"Oh, this is Aubrey," the woman said.

There was no attempt in either of them to hide the East End fruity accent in their voice. As far as Aubrey was concerned, he would have liked just a little more finesse, especially from Zena's father, who now came smiling into close-up with outstretched, bloody, feathery fingers. "Oh, you're the nice young—youngish, sorry. No offence. You're the one Zena's gone on about. Sit. That's right. Don't be fright. Like a bit of fruit or a drink? Something very special." He winked the sort of wink that men persist in winking at other men.

Aubrey did not reply but stood there sniffing the place. One could always rely on the smell of places and people.

"Sorry about the smell of prunes. They linger you know," the woman said.

"Sit down. Please sit down." The man waved the chicken as well as his hand, indicating the exact spot where they wanted him placed for scrutiny.

"I've heard a lot about you both, from Zena." Aubrey sat and wondered where the hell Zena had vanished to. He cleared his throat. "I've heard a little about you from Zena. She told me all about you."

"Then you won't approve." The man laughed until tears came to his eyes.

Aubrey had felt cheated when he first realised her parents were there, but now he felt somewhat relieved. It was quite difficult to put on a good sexual performance with too much cherry brandy coursing through the blood stream.

The chain pulled a few times out in the passage, the waters flushed, and Zena came bounding in. "Well, how are you all getting on? Mummy, please put down that book."

"No, Zena, books are sacred. I approve very much of books."

"Might I enquire which author?" Aubrey asked.

"It's War and Peace by a Russian called Tolstoy who wasn't an anti-Semite," Zena's mother said, tearing herself away for a moment. "I've been trying to read this book for two years, on and off."

"I have heard it's one of the best books ever written. I've decided to read it when I am winding towards my forties." Aubrey smiled across at her.

"Please don't think I'm rude but I must finish this page. Then I'm all yours. Morry's a good boy, he'll be sociable while I'm away." She departed immediately for Holy Russia. And Morris Conway returned to his plucking.

"Aubrey. Here a mo." Zena was imagining herself in the living role of Cleopatra. It was obvious from the way she beckoned from where she sprawled.

Being magnanimous, he joined her on the sofa

where an album of snapshots revealed all the mysteries of Cliftonville.

He could barely bear the agony, the agony of seeing Zena almost bare upon the sands of yesteryear.

"Mummy and Daddy are not too bad are they?" Zena whispered.

"I think they are charmingly naïve," he replied, desperately trying to suppress a yawn.

She stroked his kneecap. "I want you to know everything about me, Aubrey."

"I have that intention." This time the yawn escaped. "Oh dear, that ramble. Country air." He yawned again.

Mr Conway sizzled the last hair of the last fowl back into the universe and turned off the gas poker.

Mrs Conway closed her book, shook her head and the heroines and heroes and endless millions of Holy Russia fell out of her eyes. Then she smiled. "I hear you're a solicitor?" she said, drawing close. "That's nice. That's very nice."

"A barrister. He's a barrister," Zena smiled as she corrected her mother. But her mother had apparently not heard.

"It's a very important profession, a solicitor," Mrs Conway continued. "I would have probably done well at law if I'd taken it up. Being a solicitor must be very interesting."

"I'm a barrister," Aubrey said emphatically, without losing his smile. But he was not cross. As if Aubrey Field could have ever contemplated being a mere solicitor.

"A barrister then. What's the difference? As long as you're happy and got your health. That's all that matters," Mrs Conway said.

"Mummy! Please! A barrister is about as high as you can go." Zena still smiled sweetly but her voice was becoming more frantic.

"Sorry, no harm meant. I'm sure he'd be good at anything."

Mrs Conway was a very sexy woman in her own way. She was fattish but good-looking, and not unlike the sort of model they sometimes use for outsize garments. Her hair was tinted silvery-blue and she smelled quite sexy. He wondered for a moment how she would look stark naked. But he put these thoughts aside. It was not a kosher thought. Not even for this time of night.

"How about a nice glass of home-made cherry brandy?" Mr Conway suddenly said.

"Oh no!" Aubrey groaned as his pickled stomach turned over and flaming pains shot to his eyes and head.

"Oh, you must, Aubrey! It's Estelle's own and it's potency is fantastic." He seemed so disappointed that Aubrey relented, even though his stomach continued to groan.

"Oh, yes please! One glass would be delightful."

Mr Conway washed his hands, went to the sideboard and returned with glasses so overflowing that the sticky red liquid ran down his fingers and dripped onto the Wilton.

"You should feel highly honoured, Aubrey. Mummy only allows certain people to drink her cherry brandy. Even the insurance man who's been coming for as long as I've been alive has never been honoured in such a way."

"I reckon she'd marry the insurance man if I died," the butcher said, as he sipped his glass with non-English audibility.

"How could you say that to me, Morry?" the woman replied indignantly. "He's not my type. Now, if you had mentioned the greengrocer, at least you'd be nearer. What with his silver-grey hair, the fervour in his voice, and the fever in his eyes. Drink up."

"Here's to all of us. And to simchas and to peace. Lochaim!"

"Lochaim!" Aubrey had already noticed that there was nowhere within reach where he could lose the small drink that would probably finish him off. "Lochaim!" he repeated, knocking it back.

But part of him remained quite lucid, and he distinctly remembered refusing more. But politely. And he definitely saw the butcher knocking back a half tumbler of the stuff.

The woman's face coagulated until she looked like a painting in the Tate Gallery. He wondered if it were possible to steal her, and for what purpose.

"Your name really Field and not Feld?" Mr Conway managed to say.

"Yes. It's been Field for as long as—fields existed, I suppose."

"Good on you, Aubrey! My name's not Cohen. It's Conway. My old man thought Conway sounded less likely to bring bombs through the letter-box. Wish I could change it back. Whoever heard of a kosher butcher called Conway?" Then he started to sing, "Oy, yoy, shicka is a goy—" but he soon lost interest in projecting his voice, probably because Zena was holding her hand over his mouth. It seemed a rather obnoxious and cruel thing to perpetrate upon one's own flesh and blood, no matter how gently it was executed.

"I'm pleased you're Jewish," Mrs Conway said.

"What else? I'm proud of it, even if I don't look particularly so."

"What? You? You look typically Jewish, I'm glad to say. So many non-Jewish people pretend they are Yiddish these days. Don't ask me why. It's fashionable to be Jewish. And it's even all the craze with our own young. They wear huge Stars of David blatantly, outside shirts, in the West End. And this you'll never believe—they even read the Jewish Chronicle on the tube during rush-hour. In England we're not number one scapegoat anymore." Mr Conway drank some more and could hardly stand upright. But Aubrey was convinced that despite the performance, alcoholism was not Mr Conway's problem. This certainty persisted like a fact of cast iron in all the chaos of his plummeting mind. He knew this fact to be a fact because drink was the problem of no Jew dead, alive or yet to be born.

"Not number one scapegoat? You mad?" his wife ridiculed.

"I don't know what I'm saying any more. Except I love you, Ess." He grabbed his wife, but she freed herself, and Aubrey thought he could just about discern the woman apologising to him, with a tribal shrug.

"Listen, we still say, 'Is it good for the Jews?' " She pointed to Zena and then at Aubrey. Zena snuggled in towards him. "But Zena says, and Cecil and Lawrence say, and all their generation say, not knowing struggle and other unmentionables, they say, 'Is it good for the Jews?' But they say it tongue in cheek, as a joke. Get my point?" Zena tried to butt in, but this time she was shushed by Mrs Conway's proud husband.

"But wait. Wait! Wait till they have kids. Our grandchildren, they'll say it straight. Just like us, Morry. They'll pass through everything, pill parties, opera, fanatics, demonstrations, sexual dramas, education hysterics, and know what? They'll sail right through and come out all nice and good and respectable. And the New Morality will be as dead as the United Nations."

"Mummy! Why you philosophising suddenly? Aubrey, your presence certainly seems to be affecting them."

"Zena, please allow her to continue. It's rare these

[145]

days to find an ordinary woman with such articulate and interesting ideas."

The appreciated woman nodded and smiled. And continued. "Yes, our grandchildren will say straight out, 'Is it good for the Jews?' And I'll cry and die happy, knowing they know that nothing changes for us."

Zena stretched and Aubrey stood up to bring the sermon to a close.

"To your tents, O Israel," the butcher sang, wrapping a boiling fowl around his head. "Why do we Jews drink, when we can't drink? We always do what we can't." But he folded suddenly slumping down into a deep leather armchair, and soon he was snoring. Aubrey wondered why Mrs or Miss Conway hadn't apologised for such a display.

"Lovely weather, isn't it, Mr Field—erm, Aubrey. Bit sharp."

"I like all weather. I prefer it to none," he replied.

"I expect your family normally go to the sun in the winter."

"No. We are a Sephardic family and have been in this fair land for many centuries, long before Cromwell. We like it here and rarely leave these shores."

"How nice to be so settled. Mind you we rarely go abroad. Too many responsibilities."

Aubrey looked at his watch. "I'm afraid ..." He yawned. "Long day ahead. Must go soon."

He hoped they wouldn't persuade him to stay. On the other hand Mrs Conway totally ignored his remark so he just had to sit there, trying to support a chiming head and listening to the woman rattling on.

"Don't get me wrong, Aubrey. Who cares if a young man isn't Jewish as long as he's decent. On the other hand, what can be decenter than a Yiddisher boy? Or a Yiddisher girl? You must agree that a nice respectable Jewish girl is right at the top of the tree.

Money cannot buy a lovely daughter, Mr Field. Only love can. Provided the one in question has got prospects."

"Of course. I concur, Mrs Conway. I'm in accord, I mean I agree."

"Thank God our Zena's fussy and refused to marry anyone. And thank God we brought her up that way. I don't even care if the one she finally accepts furnishes her a rubbish heap, as long as it's comfortable. As long as she's happy who cares? Mind you, I don't mean a rubbish heap exactly. As long as he's respectable, sincere, and can persuade her to keep a nice Jewish home. Then I would approve, which means we approve."

"Goodnight, Mrs Conway. Thank you." He managed to hoist himself vertical and he sailed towards the door.

"Goodnight. Mind how you drive." Mrs Conway showed them the dark passage, smiled and closed the door. Aubrey could hear her gently calling her snoring husband.

"After all, why isn't he married if he's such a good catch?" Morry boomed over loudly as he returned to the world of the living.

"Shush! They'll hear." The man moaned and mumbled incoherently either a rebuke or an apology.

"Go back to sleep, Morry. Your snoring will cause less trouble."

Morry obliged and Estelle sighed as she settled down again into her armchair and probably her paperback, which, give her her due, must have weighed as much as a small boiling fowl, and she seemed determined to devour every last bit of it.

Aubrey and Zena were so completely in the dark that he yawned silently as he held on to her.

"You hold me so nicely, Aubrey. Only a strong man could afford to act so gently."

[147]

"Yes. I must go home soon."

"Are you sure you're not too tired? You seemed about to collapse inside. But then I suppose you drive yourself hard for the sake of justice."

"Yes. The Blind Goddess. An exacting mistress." She giggled.

"I really must go, almost at once, unfortunately," he said, trying not to breathe in the essence of her flesh and perfume. Not that anything except splints could have made an appreciable difference to the growth of Goliath.

"Why must you go home so soon?" Her mouth was now so close to his, but he could not move one more inch towards her.

"Yes. Yes, I must go. I must because even I am—human."

"Aubrey! Darling. How I admire you. How I respect your restraint."

"One tries one's best."

He suddenly wondered if he would even make the car at the kerb.

Then their mouths met and she started to breathe heavily.

"Aubrey. We mustn't. We must be patient." But her pressing thighs spoke another language.

"You're a very passionate girl," he whispered. "And if I do not go we shall be lost."

"I know," she replied. "With you I go to pieces. I trust you and it's just as well. But I truly admire such self-control. I've met a few men. One or two; but you, Aubrey, are quite unique."

"Zena! Zena!" Mrs Conway was calling from the frozen plains of Russia. "Zena! It's getting late."

"Coming! Goodnight, my darling Aubrey. I'm in your hands. Be nice to me. You have the power to melt me to your will. Thank you for restoring my faith in the male element of mankind. I'm longing to see you as soon as— Drive slowly, and don't get killed."

He managed to open the door and slowly negotiated the street.

"Aubrey!" Zena was calling him. He turned and she walked over to him.

They stood looking into each other's eyes, and Stamford Hill slipped away. "Aubrey—I—I don't really know who you—are."

"Oh?" he replied, coolly. "Who knows who anyone really is?"

"I know this sounds silly, but sometimes I'm afraid of—"

He placed his outstretched hands upon her shoulders, which were just waiting to be clutched. "I don't understand, Zena."

"Sometimes you don't fit together. Sometimes you are not what you appear to be." She smiled but still seemed concerned. "Sorry. I'm stupid. I don't know what I'm saying. Forgive?"

"Zena, my love, you are perfectly correct. Man is not what he is but what he thinks he can be. A man is more than he is."

"Darling, you're wonderful. That's exactly what I meant."

"Anyway, if I am so unknown, just remember how you despise all those—one or two—you've known."

"You're right. I must expect you to be different." She pecked his cheek quickly and then she ran back inside.

Aubrey was afraid to walk towards the car, so he sprinted, having once heard that this was the best means of dealing with a tightrope. And he made it to the machine and climbed in, turning towards her window. Then, waving with the back of his outstretched arm, he drove away with as much noise and speed as he could muster; so that if he should die, the newspapers would tell her that at least he was no coward, even if they did call him a lying embezzler.

But only too soon he safely returned to sickly familiar streets.

Aubrey parked his Elan and walked along the streets that were more thick with ghosts than all those long sticky fly-papers that were once so thick with flies. Within a few days of being hung up they became covered by a dying multitude of the struggling creatures. A few always seemed to stay alive a little longer than the others, continuing to kick and kid themselves they would escape the common destiny. But there was no escape.

"If I put up a sticky ghost paper tonight, Id have thick ghost jam tomorrow." A cat arched itself upon a wall; he stroked it and did not have the slightest wish to grab its throat and stop it breathing. So he stroked it again and walked on. But now he thought of Leah and wondered how to avoid her if she was still up. He was sure she was. If only he could have crept upstairs tonight, crept down tomorrow, and disappear forever. But at the very worst he knew that he'd have to brazen it out. "Just a few more days please?" he asked himself and punched his palm. But even if she did know all, could she, or any mother, send such a loving son to prison? For maybe five years hard labour? Not even a terrible mother would do that. And Leah was one of the finest mothers in the world. Thus encouraged, he continued the few steps towards his door which was just a few feet away now.

He could just imagine the hysteria. His long absence would have caused Leah to be beside herself by now. "But at least, if she's beside herself she won't be alone."

He entered the house and sure enough she was there.

Leah nodded. And nodded. "Hello. You came back then." She spoke casually but she did not fool him for one moment. She was a very subtle woman, after all she was his mother.

He did not reply except with a yawn, and he hobbled past her and clomped up the stairs, hoping she would not feel that he did not love her any more.

Thinking of absolutely nothing, he took off his clothes and dropped them on to the floor. Then he fell upon the bed which had been promising to fall to pieces for a long time. "Bed! I say! Silly bugger! Listen! Who'll collapse first and be chucked away?"

But the bed didn't reply. It just lay there like an old whore, creaking, open and waiting for his custom.

Pretty soon his eyes started to drop everything that existed in the world. And Aubrey Field hurtled down toward the dark endless fields of uncomplicated sleep. Down and down he dropped and dropped, and he was extremely grateful.

17

Next morning when Aubrey awoke and returned to earth it was still dark. Glad that the hangover had died without trace, he jumped out of bed and felt absolutely marvellous; and then he undressed. Today he was really going to spruce himself up in gay clothes befitting his inauguration.

Aubrey loved waking up before everyone else. Any action that underlined his difference from the herd was to be pursued. So he was naturally grateful for his unique metabolism, which separated him from most other mortals who needed more than a few hours' sleep. It had always been a source of self-wonder that a cat-nap thoroughly refreshed him.

He whistled as he re-dressed, and then he went downstairs. It was early enough to get away before his mother confronted him with unnecessary questions. Questions that would cast a shadow on such an important day.

Leah was there, pottering around the kitchen. At first he was surprised to see her about so early, but then he decided he wasn't really surprised. She was capable of anything. And although he was feeling on top of himself, he decided that communication with such a suspicious woman was to be avoided like the

Black Death. Nevertheless he knew he would have to throw a few words at her. "You're up early."

"Early? I'll be up early until it's too late and they put me down. What do you mean? What's early?" She clasped her concerned face between the palms of her hands, swaying in her melancholy.

"Bring me breakfast." His clipped, demanding tones were at last achieving the right balance. For years he had worked for this and now it all fell into place quite naturally.

He crumpled up the Daily Mirror, and rubbed his shoes briskly.

"What do you want to eat, Aubrey?"

"Starving. Cornflakes, kippers, scrambled eggs on toast. And cherry jam."

"Cornflakes for supper?" She clasped her open mouth.

His mother was a mad woman; there was no escaping the fact. She was stark raving mad and every moment she was getting madder. Aubrey felt an overwhelming wave of compassion sweeping through him, but unfortunately it did not stop him shouting, "BREAKFAST, YOU STUPID OLD COW." Then he said silently to himself, "I'm sorry, but I must jolt you back to earth, poor Mother."

"Do you know what's the time?" She spoke softly, as if to a little child.

"Time? Who cares about time?" He wondered why she didn't consult her own wrist. Maybe she thought that a glance less was more economical. He looked at his watch. "It's time for early breakfast. It's six-thirty."

"It's six-thirty all right. Six-thirty in the evening."

"You're a liar, you liar."

She came up close. "You're feverish. But I won't let them take you away."

Then he noticed the shop was open, and Auntie Beattie was there, chewing and humming and reading

Vogue magazine as she sat on an upturned lemonade crate.

"Evening? Why didn't you wake me?"

"You look so peaceful when you're asleep, and so nice. I didn't have the heart to bring you back into this world. I'll get you breakfast, even though it will probably be Viennas and chips."

Aubrey tried not to rush to the 'phone. "No. I'll be late. Got to go somewhere." But as soon as the dialling finished, his overstrung voice unwound into mellowness, and his taut face subsided to a smile. "Hello, may I speak with Zena?" he cooed softly, looking round at his mother who watched him from the kitchen door before retreating back to her stove.

"Hello! Zena! It's me. I shall see you there. The Wyckham Hotel, about eight. And Zena, I am taking over. Have no fear. I have everything and other things planned as well." He clicked off and swivelled his head to make sure Leah had not crept within earshot, before he spoke to himself, "I just must get that launching pad from Gregory Cohen, for the defoliation of Miss Z. Conway. But only after I am President of the S.O.S., and succumb to her raving demands."

Aubrey made for the street door.

She smiled as she went over to him. He had never seen her saunter before. "Going out again?"

"Certainly," he replied, putting on his overcoat.

She gave a nod as old as Jericho. He wondered if she knew the whole story of how he was forced to forge the cheque to release his rightful money from the vaults of perfidious Albion. "Can I assume you know everything, Mother?"

"Yes, Aubrey, I know everything."

Of course she could have been referring to the usual mystical cul-de-sacs of human emotions, for which broadminded mothers were often notorious in both fiction and in life.

But it was more than possible she was referring to the bank business. He would have liked to have spared her the painful truth for a few days longer. Because he could not bear her suffering. Not after all she had sacrificed on his behalf. And she would see him far from Whitechapel, and would rejoice again, having become aware of his entire plan for real freedom.

Yes, he would probably be languishing somewhere in the Bahamas no longer than this weekend, with Zena.

By then he would have made her extremely happy, outside wedlock, but only because of her perpetual nagging insistence. And once he had done homage to her needs, she would feel enslaved, and follow him wherever his mood happened to take them. And only sin would wipe out sin, but who was he to argue? The Bahamas, so be it.

"Goodbye then. Cancel the Daily Mirror."

"At last. Goodbye Aubrey."

"Thank you for everything."

"Don't mention it." She held the plate of Vienna sausages and chips which she had prepared for his last late breakfast. She was extemely considerate. He hoped she would die peacefully. He did not wish to appear inconsiderate but decided that he wasn't hungry after all.

Leah shrugged, went to the table, sat down, poured tomato sauce all over the food and then she pretended to eat.

Aubrey left the house rubbing his face to make sure he was alive.

His stubble proved that this was no dream. He was walking out of Hessel Street for the last time. He slowed his brisk pace, stopped walking altogether, and regarded his face in a shop window. He liked what he saw.

Even his face had changed, for what with all the things that had happened during the past few days he had forgotten to shave. Now he looked at the handsome bearded brute before him.

"Aubrey, you look even better than your father."

He swung down the street, pretending to hold a silver-topped cane, and jutting his new-born beard up towards the sky. He hoped he might get a glimpse of his father before he reached the main road.

But the clouds were far too low and Father was probably soaring high above the earth, his whirring moustache carrying him with migrating swifts, soaring south unseen towards the sun.

The dark low sky followed Aubrey all the way from East One to North-West Three, and when he reached Avenue Road he completely lost interest in anything above the tasteful bricks that comprised his very own mansion.

He opened the huge iron gate and sauntered along the drive. The sparkling Daimler was standing there. But Aubrey's Gregory Cohen was not polishing the bodywork or even gently scratching flecks of mud off with his fingernails.

All the lights were on in the house, and Aubrey stood under a slightly opened window whistling the one tune that linked a chauffeur to a barrister: the "Hatikvah", the national anthem of the Jews.

But this had no effect, so he walked right around the house and whistled the melodious air twice over. Then he tried a few less august Jewish numbers, including "My Yiddisher Momma", "Tzena, Tzena", and even that most beautiful tear-jerking "Rozhinkes mit Mandlen". All this should have done the trick, for he even clapped hands slowly as he sang the plaintive songs in a language almost as dead as Latin.

His voice rose high, clear and beautiful into the cold night. Yet he was not dismayed, indeed he was glad to be singing for the benefit of all the residents of St. John's Wood.

[156]

But in the house nothing stirred; not even the slightest bird from behind twenty identical drapes of sunflower and machine cogs, a most unusual wedding, arranged no doubt by Heals who were hardly ignorant of the latest trends.

Aubrey banged hard on the door, punishing it with the brass bear's-head door-knocker.

A man came, a sort of human being. "What you want?" The man spoke like he had a whole mouthful of jagged herring-bones.

"I am Aubrey Forbes-Levy. *The* Aubrey Forbes-Levy. Please tell Gregory Cohen I have come to claim my four walls and a floor. Thank you, my good man."

The lopsided smile loomed so close that Aubrey could smell the garlic and borsht from his mouth. With such a face the man should have been riding with Yul Brynner in his new Siberiascope production of Ivan the Not So Terrible.

"I must see the chauffeur. Gregory! Gregory the Cohen who drives." Aubrey made the motion of turning a steering wheel.

"Ah! Diabolo Juggler. Wait." Aubrey noticed the thickness of the man's hands as he slammed the door. He whistled "The Red Flag", and "Ah, Sweet Mystery of Life", and "Moscow Nights", until there came the rosy polished smiling face and open hands of Gregory Cohen. "Good evening, comrade. Can I help?"

"Gregory! At last. I must have my room or my money back."

"Room? Money? I do not see you before."

"Gregory! Stop kidding."

"Pliss. You are seeking asylum in piss-loving Soviet Union?"

"Why do you carry on not knowing me? I am Aubrey Forbes-Levy. I transacted a deal with you."

"How do you do? And goodbye." The chauffeur tried to close the door. Sometimes Aubrey could muster up the strength of a dozen men. But this was not one of those occasions.

"You conned me. How could you? A Yiddisher boy acting like this to another?" Aubrey just managed to keep the door from closing completely.

"Yiddisher? What's Yiddisher?" Gregory opened the door a little more.

"Gregory, take pity upon me. I must see my room, the room you leased me for immoral practices."

"If you do not go at once, Mr Ford Audrey, I shall call your police."

Aubrey slowly walked backwards away from the front door, and made a dash for the side door, which was supposed to lead to his room for sin. The chauffeur did not chase him. And Aubrey was relieved, if breathless, when he entered the house.

About one hundred people quietly danced under chandeliers. The accompaniment was provided by a gramophone emitting "Alexander's Ragtime Band". Most of the dancers had fixed expressions of joy welded onto their faces. All moved exactly and stiffly in a clockwise fashion round the huge mirrored room, under a rotating red-mirrored ball.

The man winding the gramophone came towards Aubrey and was joined by another refugee from Madame Tussaud's. Both identical serge suits sported a red badge showing the hammer and sickle. Aubrey concluded it was time to advance back to the safety of nearby England. The music started to run down, and the dancers danced slower and slower, until they and the music stopped entirely. The two men with ice-packed eyes walked on either side of him, towards the gate.

"Your chauffeur! You must watch him. He's Jewish."

They looked round at Gregory Cohen, who was

rubbing the Daimler but glancing towards them out of the corner of his eye.

"Ye. He's definitely a yid. He told me. Check if you don't believe me."

"A yid? You are saying that Comrade Gregor Kolchak is a tzid?"

"I'm only going by what he told me. Secretly."

"Impossible. No embassy staff anywhere outside Soviet Union is allowed to be Jewish unless he slipped through. Although, of course, discrimination is unknown in Soviet Russia."

"Gentlemen, as a card-carrying British Comrade" —he patted his jacket where his inside pocket should have been—"I can only say that one Jew has hoodwinked your security forces. But if you do not think those cunning, imperialist Jews can plant even one—"

They seemed to lose interest in what Aubrey was saying. They released Aubrey and he entered the streets of England. They quickly closed the gate, walked towards the shrubbery, where they smoked and quietly conversed.

"Goodbye, Gregory Cohen. Love to the Lubianka. Thanks for the information. I shall send your urgent message direct to Moshe Dayan, Tel Aviv."

Aubrey was shouting through the ironwork gates, and he noticed Gregory was not smiling any more. Instead he was intently watching the reflections of his two comrades in the gleaming surface of the Daimler. Then he turned towards them and laughed and shrugged. The machines of flesh merely smoked by the rhododendron bushes and stared back at Comrade Kolchak. Then they went briskly into the house.

"And if they don't get you, rest assured one of these nights I'll come with six-inch nails to decorate the exterior of your beautiful car. Either way it will be the salt mines. Goodnight Gregory Cohen." He waved at the fat man, who stood for a moment gazing at space as if it were a crystal ball revealing the future of all Soviet chauffeurs who claimed to be Jewish and later tried to deny it all.

Then just in case they had already surrounded the suspect chauffeur with invisible listening devices: "Whatever they do, Greg, remember you are a Cohen. And remember all your information will bring you a Star of David. Posthumously."

Comrade Gregory rushed inside the house and Aubrey would have danced all the way to St. Marylebone had he not the fear of being picked up by the gentle London Police for behaving in a most disorderly manner.

18

The extraordinary session of the S.O.S. had been in progress for twenty minutes, and Councillor Hetty Solomons, the guest speaker from Hove, had been speaking for only fifteen minutes. Yet it appeared she was actually coming to the point. Aubrey was delighted. He liked speakers to talk about the subjects that were advertised. Councillor Hetty's discourse had been headed "Zionism and the Pill".

"I am in favour of the pill in England. But, I must stress, I am not in favour of the pill in Israel."

"Why not?" some loud mouth interrupted and was shushed by practically the whole of the audience.

"That is a good question, and I am glad you asked it." Councillor Hetty sipped some water before continuing: "In Israel the birth-rate is not high enough. There can be no ease in Zion until we have swelled the valley and planted our progeny in the deserts."

But despite the fascinating and controversial subject, Aubrey was becoming impatient as Councillor Hetty droned on. "But here in England the pill is necessary. I am not advocating indiscriminate use of it amongst any of you who are yet unmarried. And I'm sure there must be a few."

The fact that she was obviously unmarried, childless, and sliding down the slippery slope on the other side of the menopause did not seem to diminish her authority or the interest of her audience.

"I repeat, indiscriminate use of anything connected with sexual love must be rejected. I know it can be hard. But I will not recommend the pill for use in Jewish organisations. However, I am sure that 'indiscriminate' is a word that could rarely apply to Jewish youth." She added, "Jewish youths of all ages."

How they longed to be indiscriminate. Not having the pill would not present many dangers for this audience. Abortionists would not grow fat and cruise to the Virgin Islands from the pockets of the S.O.S.

"But again I stress—in Israel it is quite different. If any of you are going there to live and you are married, or hoping to, please leave your pills behind."

If she loved the bulging belly of Zion with such passion what was she doing in Hove? Then again, it didn't matter for her. At her time of life nothing could assist her personal problems, not the pill, nor anything else. The only thing Councillor Hetty was fit for was civic responsibilities.

Aubrey whispered into Zena's erotic earhole, "I shall get you a kosher pill." Zena giggled, yawned and looked at her watch. At that moment Councillor Hetty stopped.

Everyone clapped and agreed that the talk had been most creative and fascinating.

The present president, Derek Moss, descended the plinth with a flushed but happy Councillor Hetty, and now he ascended again, clapping the illustrious guest with the rest of the audience. He thanked her profusely and at length, and his summing up of Councillor Hetty's contribution looked like lasting almost as long as Councillor Hetty's discourse.

Aubrey was therefore most relieved when a man's voice, from the row behind, started using his ear as a confessional.

[162]

"I would like to meet you, privately." The voice spoke with an intimacy that suggested unpalatable things. Aubrey did not turn to look at the owner but pondered upon the geographic origin of such a voice, and what on earth the nature of such a request could possibly be. But it helped to pass the time whilst Derek Moss droned through the announcements of events past and things yet to come, "Please God!"

But then Derek Moss announced the coffee break, and everyone vacated their chairs, and they remarked that Derek Moss had made a very clever speech as they made their way towards the aroma and the steam.

Aubrey was well aware that the man who wanted him for something or other was right behind and almost breathing down his neck.

Zena took his arm when they reached the coffee room and Aubrey noticed that all eyes were fixed upon the two of them.

"Stay here, my dove. I shall bring you coffee." He patted her hand and she smiled; then he walked into the crowd, feeling a little like Moses as it opened up before him.

When he reached the coffee table, Aubrey noticed that the mysterious little man was still clinging to him, hooking him with his bloodshot, demented brown eyes.

Aubrey looked down upon his hunter. "How tall are you?" This was the sort of question to make any normal maniac shrivel.

"Actually I'm five foot two and a half inches. In height," came the rapid reply.

"Why do you boast?" Aubrey boomed back directly, with courage.

"All right! So I'm five foot two inches. Coffee? It looks like cocoa and smells like tea." The man offered Aubrey two cups of steaming instant. Aubrey smiled through his teeth. "How did you know I needed two cups?"

A knowing smile and a shrug was the reply.

Aubrey made his way back to Zena, but this time the sea of faces would not open for him. They were obviously too anxious for coffee.

He reached Zena, who smiled serenely, took the coffee and carried on chatting to an unexploded ball of passion who wore a mini mini skirt as if challenging anyone who dared to remark that it did not become a rather fattish lady over forty-five.

Aubrey could hear the man breathing rather heavily behind him, so he turned to put an end to it.

The man wore a black corduroy suit that had been well cut, and even though the cuffs were frayed he still managed to look dapper; possibly because one's attention went naturally to the neck, which sported a mauve cravat, flamboyantly tied upon a narcissus-yellow shirt.

Aubrey did not like the man and he could see that the man knew the moment of truth had arrived. "Who are you?"

"Who is anyone?"

"What do you want?"

"What does anyone want?"

"What do you do?"

"You mean tonight?" A certain expectation lit up his eyes.

"No. I mean for a living."

"Would you believe me if I said I was a doctor of philosophy?"

"Why? Are you?"

"No. Actually I'm a student of life."

Aubrey shook the little hand that the man suddenly offered. "How do you do?" Aubrey yawned, hoping that the man would move away.

"Very well thank you. How do you do?"

Aubrey was feeling quite tense by now and was pleased that the Slightly Older Setters had finished

[164]

their coffee and that most were back in the main hall with an electric hush hovering above them.

He made his way back, with Zena, and each face watched them until they sat down, and even after: but Aubrey never lost his expression of calm humility. And this oblivious exterior was not even disturbed when Zena's thigh greeted his in a language far more voluble than words.

"I am very interested in you, and your obvious progress upward. Later I shall tell you about my propositions." It was the voice again, closer this time and more urgent.

"Who is he?" He slowly nudged Zena.

"I was just going to ask you," she mouthed back. "Never seen him before."

Aubrey turned to face the face again. "Are you a member of this society?" He himself had been a member of the S.O.S. for such a short while, but this was quite beside the point, and he did not feel that his indignation was out of place.

"Actually, I want to speak with you about all this. And other things. Later." Mr Whoeverhewas smiled as he clutched and squeezed Aubrey's shoulder with such familiarity. Lesser men would have shuddered.

Aubrey shivered, but this was entirely due to Derek Moss solemnly gavelling the already hushed audience to quiet.

Zena squeezed his hand. "You'll do it." She always suggested all sorts of other things whenever she spoke.

"You gave me the confidence," he whispered right into her ear.

"I did not. You had confidence already. You were born confident."

"Yes. Possibly you are right." He looked back to the rostrum where Derek Moss dabbed his sweaty forehead as he sought for words.

[165]

"There have been some rumours about the need of my resigning as President of this society—" No one shouted "Shame" or "Nonsense". "All sorts of disquieting rumours have come to my ear recently. One in particular concerns our new member, one Aubrey Field. It has been whispered that he should replace me in this office. Possibly I am mistaken. I hope so. And yet— As you know, I am a very busy man. A man overloaded with more than enough. If you do not want me as your President unequivocally, I would be the first to gladly step down from office. Therefore I suggest an immediate referendum so that all rumours shall cease and that I either continue with the burdens of office, a task which I have always felt honoured to undertake, or that I continue with a mere thousand things to do, instead of a thousand and one. Let us proceed—"

The rest of his speech was drowned in a great storm of applause but Derek Moss was determined to speak his last.

Aubrey hated the man up there, but it was nothing personal. Moss had the sort of face and profession that always made him want to vomit. Aubrey did not know why he hated accountants so much. He was sure there were good and bad of all sorts. He was perfectly prepared to admit that he was probably prejudiced in this respect. His hatred for the abacus-boys was absolutely irrational. But human beings were made like that. This was the sort of horrid fact about people that made people quite beautiful.

"There will be a show of hands." Moss was trying to shout, but Aubrey only got the message by lip reading.

Everybody in the hall looked towards Aubrey, and all of them were rising and clapping their hands just as if they were greeting royalty. Perhaps they wanted him to dance the Hora or something. Perhaps this was the way Presidents of the S.O.S. accepted office.

Derek Moss had given up the attempt at address- ing the congregation. There could hardly have ever been a show of hands such as this, and Moss sat gazing into the palm of his own hand lost in deep Jewish sorrow. But Aubrey could just see Moss's eyes flicker- ing about. No doubt he was all ready to spring towards the exit and make his exodus from St. Marylebone, forever.

Zena burned into his flesh. "You've done it. You've done it." She spoke with a sexual staccato. "You've done it. You've done it."

It was a walkover. It was all over bar the shouting, and now the shouting started.

"WE WANT AUBREY! WE WANT AUBREY!"

"FOR AUBREY'S A JOLLY GOOD FELLOW— AUBREY'S A JOLLY GOOD FELLOW—AUB- REY'S A JOLLY GOOD FE—EL—LOW—AND SO SAY ALL OF US."

He ascended slowly, with fantastic dignity up- wards toward the desolate figure of Moss, and walked straight over to him. "Do not despair, Derek Moss. All is not lost. There are plenty of other societies." He offered his hand, but it was no use. Derek Moss did not hear. He just stood up and stared for the last time at his audience.

"I will not even put this to the vote. I have already decided that owing to the pressure of work I must resign." He spluttered on for a few moments and then stumbled down the stairs and hurried to the back of the hall.

Aubrey turned to face his flock, and the trans- fixed assembly looked up at him with one face—the face of thankfulness.

Aubrey raised his hands and lowered his eyes. "I am truly humbled by your decision this evening. I

[167]

think you have made a wise choice, and it will be my pleasure to take you forward into the future."

He tried to continue speaking, but the little man who had been pestering him stood upon his chair and raised a pointed finger to the roof as if about to declaim the first coming of a messiah. But Aubrey could not let anything interrupt his moment. "As a barrister I am familiar—"

"Lies! Lies! He's telling you all lies," the man shouted, and then he started to sprint towards the platform. "Lies! Lies! He's a tobacconist."

So the man had not been a student of life after all. Obviously he was Mr Samuel Fineberg of the Samuel Fineberg Detective Agency.

"Lies! Lies! He's a liar! Take no notice!" The little man jumped on to the platform. "A barrister he says? He looks after a sweetstuff shop," he shouted, "His mother's shop. Leah Feld, in the East End."

Strangely enough, this interruption had not been totally unexpected. He was more numbed than surprised, and although he felt tremendously worried, deep within him he wanted to laugh.

The detective shook his head right up close to his, then, ruffling his hair affectionately, turned to the audience and shrugged and pointed towards him.

Everyone went incredibly quiet but Aubrey suddenly was unable to suppress his laughter. It became uncontrollable and infectious. Soon everyone in the hall except the detective and Zena had succumbed to the virus.

Zena stood in the front row. All her fingers in her mouth. He guessed she was not sharpening her nails to draw his blood because tears streamed from her eyes, and two black mascara rivers flowed beyond her nostrils. It was incredible. She seemed to actually believe the little man.

Zena the undone. Zena of the unred sheets. Zena

with an uncut jewel between her thighs. Zena, who only allowed a proper valuation if you signed in advance your intention to buy and use no other commodity for the rest of Jewish very mean time.

Would this be a night to relate to her grandchildren? This loss of true love? Would this indelible, despairing moment live as long as Zena?

The laughter eased and everyone was waiting for action. There was a silence so absolute that Aubrey could hear the thumping of his heart.

It was an Agincourt silence.

"My lords, gentlemen and ladies, I am going to tell you the whole truth. So don't help me by interrupting. Just listen" the little man boomed as loudly as a Major Domo.

There was never a captive audience more willing to not escape. There was never a Jewish gathering more silent.

Aubrey sidled close to the man and sniffed at his face. "A meths drinker. Poor soul. Perhaps the only meths drinker in the whole of the Diaspora."

"Throw him out," someone shouted. "Disgrace."

Aubrey raised his hands for silence. "Or, to be charitable, possibly he's an out-of-work Yiddish actor, hired by some enemy to thwart my victory."

Everyone laughed with relief and a storm of applause broke out.

"Leave, sir, leave before I turn you over to the Metropolitan Police for attempting to disturb a democratic election."

The little man went purple but did not burst as he jumped like a three-year-old off the platform.

He was given a slow hand-clap as he hurried out of the place.

Aubrey continued his presidential address and his eyes swept along the rows of smiling, thankful faces.

Only Zena did not seem totally convinced.

19

The S.O.S. had departed for Hendon, Willesden, and North Finchley. And Aubrey watched Zena as she watched the last member leave the hall. And still she had not uttered a solitary word.

"Who was that man?" She broke her silence as he took her arm and led her up the stairs and out of the place.

"I can honestly say I never saw him before," he replied.

But this did not seem to please her. Even her flesh did not seem to give to his touch, yet he was far from depressed because Zena was not like the others. This was the reason he had chosen her for himself. She did not run with the herd.

"You must trust me," he said as the cold night air hit them in the face.

Yes, Zena was able to think for herself and there was no doubt at all in his mind that he would easily win her round.

Then he saw her.

Leah! Huddled against the closed doorway of a dry cleaners. There was no mistaking her. Or him. The student of life, otherwise known as Fineberg, detective, who stood a few yards from his mother, holding on to a parking meter and smoking furiously.

Both watched Aubrey and Zena as they approached.

There was simply no avoiding them, so Aubrey clutched Zena tighter and quickened his step towards the showdown. Only tuneless breath escaped from his pursed lips when he attempted to whistle a Viennese waltz.

Leah stepped out from her doorway and stood in the middle of the pavement.

"Look! There's your little man. The one you don't know," Zena said as Fineberg joined Leah and also stood before them, barring the way.

"I don't know this woman." Aubrey's voice floated upon the taut air as Leah stepped forward and spoke directly at Zena.

"Don't believe this man because he is not a man. He is my son. And he is not a barrister, he is a tobacconist. He doesn't live in St. John's Wood, he lives in Hessel Street, E.1., Whitechapel. And he has never been more than five yards away from me in his life before. Except recently. Though I even prayed for him to go."

It was not her words that made Aubrey see it was useless. It was the realisation that Zena was actually believing that this woman was speaking the truth. That really hurt. The fact that it was the truth was surely beside the point. And now Zena was swallowing Leah's improbable truth, hook, line and sinker. And he would be lost without a trace.

"I supported Aubrey all his life and this is the way he treats me. And he's not only a liar, he's a gunof. He embezzled a motor-car and an entire wardrobe from Harrods of Knightsbridge, London S.W.1. But I forgive you, Aubrey. I just don't want you telling lies and living what you ain't." She turned again to unblinking Zena. "Maybe *I'm* mad. A mother's love is always mad, because there's no reward except this

[171]

sort of reward; a pain in the head, a pain in the heart and a pain in the pocket."

"I verify all this dear lady is saying. I am a private detective. My name is Samuel Fineberg. Not only the finest but also the best. From North East, North West and even Up West. And my charges are reasonable. You can find me in the 'phone book. I tracked this poor boy down in no time." He handed Zena a card. "If ever you need, my estimates are free."

Aubrey continued smiling but it was the smile of someone who knew all his dreams were about to die. Zena would believe them and they would take him home and he would never see her again.

Leah started again. "You look a nice girl—so I'm telling you straight. My Aubrey is a little bit meshugger, but harmless. He has never harmed one hair on my head. So far."

Fineberg stood behind them now and Aubrey turned to growl at him, but the little detective patted Aubrey's shoulder. "Nothing personal, Aubrey. An assignment. Let's be friends; you need me."

"Zena, please say something. Say you don't believe them," he pleaded, pouring all his sincerity into her impassive eyes.

"Mind you, I don't want you to think my Aubrey's not good enough for you. Or anyone. He's fifty times better than most other men; even if I do say so myself. It's just that I couldn't bear the deception and I don't like liars. In fact I hate them. And who wants to hate their own son?"

"No one!" cried the almost crying Fineberg.

"What I don't understand—" Leah's voice changed tone as she repeated the line—"What I don't understand is why a lovely girl like you ain't married already and is wide open to all and sundry. Such customers like my Aubrey you can live without."

Zena managed to manufacture a sweet smile.

"Don't take it too hard, son. An assignment's an assignment. You've got a lovely mother there." Aubrey saw the hungry gleam in Fineberg's eye as he looked over the length and breadth of the Feld. "After all, an assignment's an assignment," the man said automatically, his mind dwelling on baser things. Yet Aubrey did not feel inclined to stand in judgment on this depraved, degenerate and despicable individual.

"Excuse me, Mother. I have a few personal things to talk over."

Leah nodded and moved a few feet away, pulling the detective with her.

"Goodbye, Aubrey," Zena said, moving off. Aubrey went after her and restrained her.

"You'd go? Just like that?"

She shrugged. "What's the point of staying longer?"

"You believe what they said?"

"Yes." There was a lot of sadness in her voice.

"What's the difference? Aren't I the same person I was a half an hour ago?"

"No." She turned to go again but he held her arm and turned her around to face him.

"Would you have wanted me if I told you I was nothing? Just another nonentity who helped his mother in a sweetshop? Be honest."

"I don't know. Maybe not. But this way certainly not. You lied to me right at the beginning. You pretended you were something other than you are. And I wanted someone different. Someone honestly different."

"I am different, Zena. Believe me. It's my—it's your—sorry. It's our last chance." Aubrey was aware of his mother and Fineberg inclining ever closer.

"I wish you were the person. Unfortunately you're not."

"He's not such a bad boy," Leah said, as she scrutinised the faces of the two of them in turn.

"It's just that I'm so tired of men who can't grow up. Please understand. I did like you enormously. Pity it was all a fabrication. Goodbye, Aubrey." She offered her hand.

"I'd change for you. I'd really change for someone like you."

"No. You'll never change. People can't. Goodbye."

He stopped his eyes filling with tears. "Goodbye, Zena Conway." She didn't affect him in the slightest any more, so there was simply no point in crying.

"Goodbye, Mrs Field," Zena said, walking away.

"Feld's the name," Leah shouted. "What a lovely girl."

"Goodbye, Aubrey. I wish you luck," Zena called back as she walked towards the main road.

"Silly cow! I'm not what I am but what I should have been, what I could have been," he shouted along the windy wet street, but Zena had already turned the corner. And he would never see her any more.

He walked with his mother through the back-streets of St. Marylebone. Fineberg held Leah's other arm. Already the detective was collecting his fee.

They all stopped for Leah to catch her breath. "Lovely fresh air." She breathed in and coughed out all the smoke from St. Marylebone Station.

"You were the shortest-lived president in history." Fineberg laughed as they neared the empty main road where the Metropolitan Line at Baker Street Station went direct to Aldgate East.

"It'll be lovely getting home again. I feel miles away," said Leah.

"Miles away from where?" The little man was puzzled so he chuckled to hide it.

"Miles away from—How do I know? Miles away from nowhere. But I'm still longing to get there."

"I can't wait." Fineberg rubbed his two unusually soft hands together.

"I'll show her. I'll show everyone." Aubrey spat at the drenching rain. "I'll change. You'll see if I don't change."

"Good. I've got some shirts ready. And now you're no longer in mourning you can shave the bum fluff off and look like my Aubrey again."

"Never. Aubrey is dead." He shivered and his teeth chattered.

"Home isn't far away. It's nice and warm there," Leah said.

"Home? Where's that?"

"Home is where you hang yourself." Fineberg nearly doubled up with laughter. "Sorry, just my joke."

Leah shook her head, accepted a sugared almond from him and waited for the traffic lights to change and then crossed the main road. Aubrey walked beside her, taking her pace, expecting no cataclysm to destroy Baker Street and rid him of his fate.

They reached the car and Aubrey clenched his eyes tight, not wanting to be reminded of his days of glory.

"Let's go by car back to the East End," the detective said, his eyes filling with tears.

"You've been driving me to my grave all your life," Leah said. "Would you like a lift back to the East End, Mr Fineberg?"

"You bet. I wouldn't say no, even in a crazy car like this."

"Good. You can drive us," she replied.

Aubrey got into the death seat and Leah sat upon his lap. Mr Fineberg did not lose his smile as he climbed inside and sat before the wheel, like he had just been given the command of the Q.E.2.

Leah giggled as the detective switched on the engine.

"Mother, I tell you, I am on the edge of the edge of a nervous breakdown," Aubrey's weedy voice wailed as he pressed his face into the familiar Astrakhan curls of her coat. He closed his eyes as the car shot away from the kerb.

"Mr Fineberg, what a magnificent driver you are."

"Why shouldn't I be? A man should do three things well. Drive well, make love well—"

"What's the third thing?"

"I ain't decided yet."

"Mr Fineberg, your collars are dirty. No one looks after you. Bring them tomorrow so that my son can put them in the machine."

Aubrey allowed his eyes to open, "Yes, Mr Fineberg, why are you thread-bare? I thought your business was thriving. It says so in the adverts."

"This shmutter is disguise," replied Mr Fineberg. "Too busy to take them off after the last job." He lit half a whiff as they drove through the night. "Do not take it too hard, Aubrey. An assignment's an assignment."

Leah sighed and smiled and sighed, and then she sang a sweet song of her Yiddish girlhood. "Gei ich mir shpatzirn, tra-la-la-la-la-la-la."

Aubrey's mind wandered over the debris of the desolate future. He would never know Zena, not in the Biblical sense, nor in any way.

"She was not for you. You weren't good enough for her. And she certainly wasn't good enough for you."

"Mother, forgive me for what I am about to say, but if you speak another word I shall plunge your false teeth right down into your lungs."

"Yes darling, but not on an empty stomach."

"I am having a nervous breakdown, can't you see? I am having a breakdown any moment now," he screamed.

"Darling! Wait until we get back to the East End. Breakdowns are nicer amongst your own surroundings."

[176]

He hated her and he wanted to kill her, and he loved her because she was right. She was always right. As usual he would follow her advice, and defer his breakdown until they were the other side of the Aldgate Pump.

20

Aubrey looked at himself in the mirror that had also seen better days. He was wasting away before his very eyes.

Yet each day had proved that miracles still happened, for each day miraculously passed.

Aubrey had not exactly kept track of time, but he knew it was barely a few Sabbaths since losing Zena. Friday nights were marked with indelible ink in his mind. This night shone out like a lone oasis in an endless desert of days.

Leah always lit the candles on Friday and went through her mumbo-jumbo of waving her hands over them whilst emitting strange shrieks for Zion. "Next year in Jerusalem" had been the fervent cry, still lingering somewhere on the air; "This year, next year, sometime, never." How often had Aubrey asked, "Why not this year in Jerusalem?"

"This year in Jerusalem? God forbid. You can buy candles also here in Whitechapel. And work just as hard." Leah never varied her reply.

He could see that he was just a shadow of his former self, and would just continue to waste away until he was completely gone. And no one noticed the deterioration except himself. He simply could not drag his eyes away from his face, his neck and his caved-in belly.

He had shrivelled and curled up inside, and there was no fight left within him. Yet he was proud of himself. Any other human being who had passed through such valleys and such shadows would now be no more than fodder for the class and non class-conscious maggots.

The shop was shuttered and the door was locked, but Auntie Beattie was there, and the sisters counted the money whilst shaking their heads at the day's taking. Those small towers of coins spread all along a back shelf. Aubrey had never known them admit that any single day had been remotely profitable, even though the till sometimes overflowed with pound notes and money spilled over onto the floor.

"Remember how much we took 23rd September, nineteen fifty-three? That was a day. Things declined ever since," Auntie Beattie said.

"Your memory, Beat! We took tuppence-farthing that day."

"Stop choking me off. She's always choking me off." Beattie nodded to the bottles of lemonade and cherryade, and her grotesque reflections nodded back.

"Why should I take anything out on you?" Leah shrugged with her mouth.

"Shut up, you two," Aubrey shouted.

Auntie Beattie bawled, "Now you too, Aubrey."

"He was just telling both of us to shut up. So shut up," Leah shouted.

"If only my hearing was A.1," Auntie Beattie replied.

"Thought it was your eyes, Auntie." He tried to be kind.

"Eyes! Ears! What's the difference? They're all no good. Tell me another person who suffers like me?"

[179]

They couldn't, so she cheered up. "Is he coming tonight? Your detective?"

"Of course. We're celebrating."

"So it's going nicely, Leah. Hope he doesn't think you've got money. Because you have. Anyway, you look nice for him."

"I'm celebrating the fact that it's the Sabbath and we're alive. And that so far my son hasn't been locked away."

"Is it safe to eat this peeled orange, Leah?" said Auntie biting deep into the juicy dome.

"No. Never know who's been handling it." Leah snatched it away. "Looks a little touched."

Auntie Beattie seemed disappointed and he felt sorry for her. "It's touched like me. Bet you wish you were touched, eh, Auntie?"

And even though Leah snarled and Auntie Beattie went the colour of beetroot, at least it passed a little of the awful time.

Aubrey rubbed the concave of his belly. "I'm so pleased it has decided to leave home. Yet I'm sorry it's not going all the way."

"We need salty water for the potatoes, Aubrey."

"Of course you're wasting away, Aubrey. You won't eat. Your strength is going, and you're following it." Leah turned to Beattie. "He's wasting away. He don't argue any more: he don't curse me like he used to. It's serious." She turned to her son. "Where has your brain gone? You can live without a heart, but where is your brain? Answer me. Not speaking doesn't become a respectable Yiddisher boy."

"I am melancholy, Mother. I have given in. You have won. I am defeated. I can never leave you." He still looked at himself in the mirror. He loved to watch his eyes when he was being dramatic.

Leah had not even listened to his reply because Fineberg came in. Whistling.

[180]

" 'S all right, ladies! You can put down your ice-picks. Look who it ain't. 'S only me." Fineberg closed the door behind him and took his coat off.

"Hallo, Leah! Hallo, Beattie!" He rubbed his palms to show that happy days were here again. "Am I late?"

"You're never late, Mr Fineberg," Leah cooed, and Mr Samuel Fineberg, detective, went humming to the busy, steaming, bustling gas-stove, lifted jumping saucepan lids and breathed in steam from the bubbling pots. Then he looked around to see if his appreciation was being appreciated. It was.

Then Fineberg went over to the unmoving Aubrey Field, whose fixed eyes watered from staring at himself.

"The main reason I come to see your mother is really to make a certain proposition to you," Fineberg whispered intimately, and Aubrey, hating his ears kissed, was instantly nauseated.

Nothing would have surprised Aubrey about the obnoxious little private dick. It was a pity he wasn't a little more private. Aubrey had seen this chassidic Casanova in action. Not entirely, of course, but enough to show which way the weather-cock was pointing. He had observed this man in action with his own mother. There was that memorable occasion of a week before when they both rolled over and over the floor whilst chewing Mars Bars. And she had actually enjoyed the episode.

Aubrey didn't know why he should have been surprised at Leah's antics. The desires of the flesh had always pervaded both sides of the family. But his own mother, he was quite ashamed to admit, probably was the most voracious member of the tribe for as long as it had existed.

Her future undertaker would have to really watch himself and make doubly sure that she was really dead,

[181]

or he'd find himself performing an unexpected duty in an unexpected bed. Leah would spring up like a jack-in-the-box when all the others had fled, and she'd open her shrouded arms and sing, "Before I go, there's something I want. Come over here. You are Jewish, aren't you? You can't beat a nice Yiddisher boy."

And the Irish digger would keep on nodding, more from fright than from a denial of his own faith.

Aubrey pushed his mind backward and tried to remember a nicer thing. He had not made a hole through his floor with a brace and bit just in order to see Fineberg trying to play upon his mother's—well, he had to face it, there was no other phrase for it— the vital organ of his mother's sexual anatomy.

Indeed, he would have been shocked, lying on the floor like that, his eye to the floorboard, braving splinters in the delicate instrument of his eye, night after night.

He had stood sentinel simply because he didn't want her takings taken.

But in watching the sickening advances of the man in advanced years, Aubrey always made sure his right eye was tightly closed, so that his mother's partly clothed matchstick legs and gristle arms were always properly covered by at least one eyelid.

So far, Fineberg had only used his fingers. So far, Leah had kept him at bay even though she giggled continuously. So far, their respective legs had certainly moved, but fortunately only independently and not towards each other.

Once she had even cried, "Fineberg! I cannot. I am too selfish. Anyway, what would Aubrey think of me?"

Aubrey looked up at the little hole in the ceiling. It was funny. Down here it looked no more than the wet dream of a fly, but up there it revealed a passion so wide in scope that only a panoramic screen could do it horrifying justice.

To change the awful subject Aubrey looked out of the window. The Lotus Elan was still there. It looked forlorn and rather like a knocked out tank dumped in the Sinai. Despite its shabby state, Fineberg had been using it for several days, and he was welcome to it. Leah had given it to him in lieu of the fee he had expected for bringing Aubrey back for the burial service of his continuing life. Once upon a time even the milkman laughed when Aubrey greeted him daily with "Where there's death there's hope." Now the milkman had no time for anyone other than the panting ladies of Tower Hamlet, who required double cream every morning without fail, from the slick-haired yogurt yencers who came and went on their silent floats, bringing long-lasting milk to short-lasting desires. Their horses had long since chased the dodos and the unicorns down streets that no longer saw the sun or snow.

Leah shoved something into their hands. "Nice piece of cheesecake? Or bread pudding? Homemade!"

Fineberg had been lucky. The Lotus Elan meant he hadn't done badly out of the transaction. No wonder his cuffs were no longer frayed, and he could afford to eat double portions of salt beef and latkes at Blooms every other night.

The car was lost to Aubrey. This had to be faced. It had gone the way of Zena and freedom, and Mr Fineberg had infiltrated his deserved world and was making ravishing strides to bring it to ashes and incarcerate the sole remaining king who ruled the empty streets from a burning throne. In other words, Aubrey knew he would be certified as soon as Leah came round to her own not so inner conviction that it would be for his own good. Not realising that the "his" in

[183]

question was the man trying to enter her number one safe and rob her of everything.

The detective held Aubrey's shoulders as he gazed out of the window. "Lovely foggy night," he said. "Undertaker weather. Listen, Aubrey, I can use in my organisation an astute Jewish feller with initiative and maybe a little to invest towards a possible partnership."

Aubrey hissed full in the face of the man who had managed to bridge two opposite worlds and thus have him banished from either. There was no turning back, but Aubrey had to feign reasonableness whilst he sought a third way out.

"Mother! I capitulate. I accept you've won."

"Won? What's winning? You embezzling from me and running away."

"You always nagged me to leave home," he pleaded.

"Yes, but not with two thousand pounds of my money," Leah replied.

"What you both talking about?" Beattie asked with a plaintive plea.

"Ah! Human nature. People and the way they're like people.

Aubrey knew there was nowhere else to go, except upstairs.

"Where do you think you're going?" Leah called softly, softly and slowly, the way one speaks to a backward child.

"To my bedroom. Up to my bed, to waste away."

"Why did you come back, Aubrey?"

"How should I know? Now you want me home; the other week you wanted me to leave you."

"To leave me, yes, but not with two thousand pounds. Yes, Aubrey. Go to bed. You're better off there. I'll bring you up a lovely hot cup of lemon tea when I find your special cup."

"And a bacon sandwich?"

"Anyway, for you and a quiet life, I'll even bring up a chicken sandwich."

Aubrey closed his eyes when he saw the mountain of stairs. She followed him out to the landing.

"I knew, Aubrey. Everything. All the time. Right from the start. Get into bed now. It looks as if you can't survive without your mother after all. Poor Aubrey!" she said. "What are men? Who are they? Where do they come from?" she asked the universe through the cracks in the ceiling.

He walked like a man in chains. Shuffling. His strength ebbing away from him. Up the stairs, up and up and up he went. "I'll show her yet. I'll still prove I can stand on my own two feet. I'll show all of them," he shouted as he clonked towards the sky; yawning upwards he allowed himself to follow his voice.

Leah shouted after him, "Not so loud, Aubrey."

"'S matter? 'Fraid I'll wake the dead?"

"I don't trust you. Go straight into bed, or they'll come and take you away."

He was not quite finished yet. Napoleon and Samson had fallen, and Goliath. History was literally littered with fallen giants. Socrates, Icarus and Napoleon had fallen. Even David had fallen after felling Goliath. There was no escape. Poets and mass murderers tasted just as sweet to the chomping chops of growing maggots. But Aubrey still had life coursing through his veins and all was not yet lost.

"You can't live without me," Leah called up the stairs. "But when I'm gone I dread to think of what will become of you."

He'd show her that it was too soon to croak his defeat. The final battle had not yet started, but tonight he was so exhausted that he fell straight down on to the bed. And then the bed hurtled down.

Tonight he would again not deign to remove his clothes. He would stay in the Harrods until it rotted

[185]

on his back. "A warrior cannot afford to remove his armour." Aubrey climbed into bed and lay down desperately trying to think—that he was nothing.

And although he was determined not to succumb to the full Nelson of Morpheus, he was equally certain that a slight closing of his heavy eyes would not be actually giving in, not setting up a precedent for the—what was that thing called?—Ah yes, he remembered now. The future.

Those two obnoxious words were the last thing his noble mind brought forth before it cracked under the strain of weightless sleep.

21

It was not a nightmare. He only had nightmares
when he was awake. This was a bad dream. The sort
you know you are dreaming and hope will soon end.

There was this sound of a party. And they knocked
back pints of his blood, calling it cherry brandy, and
he reluctantly supplied his own private source of electricity to illuminate the whole dark endlessness of
hell.

Aubrey lay stretched out ready for the shroud. His
mind had gone beyond the point of no return. He felt
no inner or outer pain when he watched his brain and
marrow-jelly being frothed up together in the Kenwood
mixer before being spread like meringue topping to
shampoo the copper hair of Auntie Beattie that came
out in handfuls whenever you pulled it.

Lavatories were the last wonderful places left in the
world. He started to pee down the hole, watching the
steam arise. Then, just as the golden stream was about
to dwindle, he pissed his initials boldly across the dis-
tempered walls. It was always amazing how he had
stored away just enough to complete his task.

There was only one other ritual that Aubrey was
compelled to observe in stink holes, piss palaces, cin-
ema cubicles and shit houses. This entailed rushing
straight away from the hole, so that he would not be

sucked down to where all the ooze of London's orifices merged to flow beneath the sweet Thames, until it reached the estuary and lost itself in the sea.

When Aubrey returned to the living-room his mind hurtled down and down. He crashed and died and opened his eyes to see Fineberg drinking the vodka of his father.

Aubrey went close to scrutinise the man and he could not stop thinking about the long underwear that Stalin must have worn. "Colour? Red, I bet. Dyed in blood."

They started dancing downstairs and the walls swayed and the cut-glass shivered and the ceiling shook like an outraged stomach.

Beattie cried for her husband.

"If you're going to turn on the water-works, flood your own nice and comfortable two-room smart maisonette."

But Beattie howled even more. "It makes me feel so much better, after," she sobbed.

Leah and the detective tangoed on to a Victor Sylvester foxtrot.

"But who are you, Mr Fineberg? I don't believe you're a detective. It's a cover! You've come from Liverpool to show her how to invest her winnings."

"What winnings? Have I won something?" Leah's eager face searched the others.

"What winnings? The money you're not telling me about." Beattie laughed knowingly. This accusation had been made often enough throughout the years, just in case one day it came true.

Even the wailing radio through the wall brought a fresh watery onslaught from Beattie's eyes.

"Why you so sad tonight, Miss Whitechapel?" The dancing detective chucked her chin as he sailed past.

"That music reminds me of the cemetery."

"Why should Moslem Bellyache Blues remind you of that?"

"What doesn't remind me of burial grounds?" She put on her hat, and then her shoes.

"Why go if you're so miserable?" Leah's words were so sweet. Each one sounded individually rolled in honey.

"Miserable? Who me? I'm happy. I'm ecstatic. Don't ask me why but I always have to go home when I feel this glow."

"Don't come too early tomorrow. And cheer up," Leah shouted. "Or you can stay here tonight, if you like."

"No, I want to go home. I always go home when I'm happy." Beattie departed, trying hard to show how hard she was trying to suppress her sobbing.

Leah glided into a quickstep as soon as the door closed. And she danced and danced and danced until dawn started poking the sky. The music of Roy Fox, Geraldo and Harry Roy became madder and madder till the detective sidled her into the kitchen, where over chopped liver sandwiches, she revealed the combination of the safe.

Unfortunately for Fineberg she gave the wrong numbers.

The ghost of Aubrey's beloved father bounced gently around the ceiling, but still managed to play clock patience.

"I would have thought there were nicer places to pass the time," Aubrey cupped his hands and gently called up to his father.

"I have no choice. I have to stay until Passover. Incidentally, Aubrey, beware the wiles of Fineberg alias Benny Meredith."

"Benny Meredith?"

"Yes. He who betrayed Trotsky from his second-floor office near Whitechapel Station, Whitechapel,

London, East One." His father pointed down with a half-munched chicken leg, straight at the traitor in the kitchen.

"That's a funny name for a Yiddisher man. Fineberg suits him."

"Yiddisher man? Him? These days its fashionable to be Jewish. Everyone wants to be newly elected to the non-victims' club. We had plenty of vacancies in 1945. Nobody applied then." The ghost flung down his finished drumstick, popped like a bubble and disappeared.

Leah and Samuel were giggling and they had reason to be gay. They had won their victory, and the dawn orgy of tickles and hot beigels freshly arrived from the All-Night Beigel Shop, was to celebrate his funeral. They were burying him in a communal grave, with all the other bachelors of Bow, Stepney and Stoke Newington; and they were dancing upside down so that Fineberg's sudden false beard wouldn't fall off.

There was a ring in the old man's hand. It reflected dawn as it came trembling over the warehouses. Leah nodded her approval of the gold band as the detective slipped it on to her claw. The red stone was as large as a gobstopper.

"My father is gone. Killed no doubt by your insatiable desire for hot beigels and passion," Aubrey bellowed at the detective and a great wave of happiness surged over him.

Then he awoke.

His bed was wet, but he was sure that it was sweat. He had stopped wetting the bed long ago. But to make sure he sniffed the sheet and was glad it only smelled of mothballs and paraffin.

He had been dreaming and he remembered practically everything that he dreamed. But there was something else, a little thing that slipped the mind.

He sat on the bed, trying to send his thoughts safariing back, deep into the reaches of his mind. Something disturbed him, something embedded in his dream that refused to be remembered.

It was bitter cold, so he placed his plum and purple dressing-gown over his Knightsbridge attire. All was silent. The tick of his pocket watch reverberated like a metronome.

What was that other part of the dream? His mind needed defrosting with coffee and then he would remember.

What was the point of remembering if Leah Feld obscured the living-room, the kitchen, the shop, the earth, the sky, the future and the past?

Yet still the unopened portion of his dream niggled at him.

He crept downstairs so as not to wake her.

The dream was over; just like his life. All would be a nightmare now.

Then Aubrey saw a strange man in the room. He went straight over to him because even at this late stage of his life he feared no one. Then he realised that the man's face was his own, himself in the mirror. Naked Aubrey, like a tortoise without a shell. All white and slimey like a soft cod's roe.

For his new beard was gone. He wasn't dreaming. He gently stuck the point of a convenient hat-pin into the soft centre of his chin. "Ouch!" No, he was wide awake. And beardless.

And then he remembered the rest of the dream.

Stroking his flabby chin he knew everything. He did not even need to turn round to find what would be there.

She would be there, as cold as yesterday's bread pudding. But he could not resist the desire to see her motionless, so he turned around, slowly.

Leah was spreadeagled on the floor exactly as he had visualised. And she was stone-cold dead.

At first he didn't believe his luck. She was dead. Leah was dead. D-E-A-D.

The semi-precious garnet impersonating a ruby, perched on her rigid finger, reflected the flickering of the coal fire in the grate. So that part of his dream was true. All his dreams were coming true.

He wanted to dance. Taking off his shoes so as not to squeak, he leaped in the air. And he danced beautifully to the Pakistani opera from next door.

So Leah was mortal after all. She was dead, so he danced and danced, because she was dead and wouldn't move any more.

He sat down on the floor quite near her and did not close her eyes because she seemed exceptionally lovely tonight.

Aubrey felt close to his mother. Not that he had ever been distant. But there was a certain nobility about her face that he had not noticed before. "You were a long time dying, Leah. But better late than never."

He made himself a nice quick cup of tea with a tea-bag, ate some of her delicious apple strudel, and then he meditated upon the nature of life and death in general and pondered upon the manner of her going in particular.

He remembered every detail. Like a spy probing into enemy territory he explored every facet of every detail. His very survival depended upon his total awareness of all the facts of her unnatural but necessary departure.

But he reckoned that all this could wait until dawn.

And although his beard was gone he was not unduly depressed. His mother's going far outweighed that loss.

He simply could not suppress his need to dance. He would have preferred piety, pity and contemplation, but sometimes one simply had to give way to one's inner feelings.

He leapt over her corpse and jumped into his shoes,

and then, after dancing around the house, opened the door, being careful to lock it again behind him. Then he danced down Hessel Street and into Commercial Road and along it. It was so unreal and stage-like, so right for feet as light as clouds.

If a cemetery had been open he would have danced upon every tombstone. "Because you are so dead, and I am still alive," he would shout to every unseen grinning skull. He shouted it to the face that floated towards him, a pink blob in the black early morning.

It belonged to a constable in uniform.

The policeman did not come close, so Aubrey danced right up to him. "Goodnight constable. Or should I say good morning?"

"'Scuse me, sir, are you feeling all right?" The uniform leaned over and held the dancing Aubrey and sniffed his mouth.

"Of course I am. I'm dancing officer."

"I can see that."

"I'm dancing because I'm not dead and the music is so sweet."

"Now look, sir, I advise you to go straight home." The policeman had an extraordinarily kind face.

"If you ignore me, officer, I shall dance out of your life, all the way to Leman Street."

"Right! On your way. I haven't seen you." And the man slowly walked away, whistling, his eyes peeled for dope-fiends, cat-burglars, female impersonators, and anarchist slogan daubers.

Aubrey pirouetted all along the deserted Commercial Road until he reached Leman Street.

But as soon as he got there he remembered Leah lying with her spring broken, on the floor. So he quickly danced all the way back towards his home again.

For Aubrey Field, demented dancer, Angel of Death,

beardless assassin, decimator of human life, or, in the simple words of Monsieur Roget's Thesaurus, 'murderer extraordinary', had many, many things to do before he could continue his dance.

22

Aubrey waltzed into his house and stood above his mother who lay exactly as he had left her; stone-cold dead in the centre of the room.

She was more beautiful than he had ever seen her before, and he could not take his eyes off her.

Kneeling beside her, Aubrey gently removed a tiny whisp of fluff from a nostril, and he was glad that her eyes were still wide open. He wanted her to see his gratitude for the clean, crisp way she had died.

He could see his own reflection in her eyes and he liked what he saw. The calm joy and serene strength that fled when Zena walked out of his life, had returned. Leah's exodus had brought all his confidence flooding back.

He was so overjoyed that tears came to his eyes and fell into her's. "I wanted you dead, I admit. But I wanted you dead and happy. You can see that now, can't you?" He laughed softly into her cold ear, and then he tugged her hair so that her head nodded upward a few times.

"Thanks! You're so understanding." Leah was certainly a mother in a hundred million. But one thing still grieved him. He knew that she did not like to think of him as her murderer. He understood though. Mothers hated to think the worst of an only son.

Of course he had helped her die, but surely a loving son was expected to do everything he could to help his mother.

Apart from his general happiness, Aubrey was relieved that at last the dream and the nightmare were over, and that his mother lay dead in the real room in the stark reality of Hessel Street.

He pulled her head upward again so that it faced the kitchen where once she had reigned, and he opened her mouth with his other hand and tried to emulate her voice through his own closed lips. "Aubrey! How you made me suffer! What was all my sacrifice for? No, don't tell me. That hundred watt bulb up there gives me more light than all your answers. Now lay me down. I am dead tired," she said.

"Certainly, Mother dear," he replied, laying her head down again, very gently.

Aubrey looked at the electric bulb, and at the table directly beneath it, from where she had apparently fallen and broken her neck.

But he knew otherwise. And any expert who cared to examine the facts more closely would soon see that it had not been as simple as all that. He was not denying that an old lady could get a sizeable electric shock from changing an electric bulb, and it was also true that she could fall and break her neck and die. But not Leah.

She was not the sort to die such a trivial death. But who would face the truth? Who was brave enough to admit that a devoted son could electrocute a loving mother without an apparent shred of mercy? And even if they did come round to the fact that he had despatched her, would they accept that he had done it only for her own benefit?

Besides, they would ridicule him and laugh when he revealed his method of terminating her. Who would be broadminded enough to believe that he had killed her with his own personal supply of electricity that he carried for lethal and loving purposes? They would laugh at the truth; that this electricity was a rare and special gift gathered from the whirring moustache of his father in the sky and from the pulsing nipples of Zena Conway of Stamford Hill.

They would be too blinded to even notice the sparks shooting from between his legs.

He gently spat upon his handkerchief to wipe away a rivulet of smut upon her forehead.

Aubrey could hear a summing up. from a really perceptive and famous pathologist: "And the said Aubrey Field suggested to his aged mother that she should bathe her feet in warm water. And when she complied and her feet were fully immersed, this so-called devoted son came from behind with high voltage live electric wires. And he stuck these lethal elements into her ears, her nostrils and other parts of the anatomy lower down. Then, without a flicker of mercy he turned on the electricity current—"

It was true that he did persuade her to soak her terribly aching feet; it was also true that she was pleased to comply. It was also true that he did attach electric wires directly from the fuse-box into her ears and nostrils.

"What you doing, Aubrey?" she said, dozing off.

"It's electric treatment, Mother, for relaxing you," he remembered that he had replied. Well it certainly did the trick and she looked so perfectly relaxed as she slept. He was pleased because he knew she would not understand the next part of the treatment. To make sure she was fully asleep he had to insert those live wires much lower down into her unmentionable regions. That's where the pathologist was way off the beam. How could he have done such a thing if she had been awake?

And now came the object of the whole exercise;

the part that nobody would believe. He was about to use his own source of interior electricity to end her misery for ever.

When she was slumped nicely and deeply sleeping, he kissed her with all the invisible electricity of his soul, and catapulted her far from this vale of sighs.

"You held me back, Mother, but at last you have the decency to let me go."

But there was just one more thing that he had to do. She had to be got rid of if he was going to enjoy his new found freedom.

He could not leave her there, in the centre of the room, no matter how decorative she looked. Leah, like other mortals, would disintegrate, and even the odour of curry and joss-sticks would not cancel out the aroma of her decomposition.

There was also Auntie Beattie and Mr Fineberg to consider. They could hardly be expected to just accept her lying there, rotting, in the middle of the living-room.

He got up from his couch, made some instant tea, and thought back over the reasons he had killed her. Not that he had any regrets, or that he would not do it again if he had the opportunity. But it was always good to be absolutely clear about one's motives, no matter how pure you knew you were, and how generous your actions, it was only fair to leave no room for doubt, especially if the person you murdered happened to be your mother.

Her jaw fell open and she seemed about to make a comment so he clasped his hand gently across her mouth.

"Mother! Listen! Before I tell you exactly why I did what I did, I want to reassure you that I will not go to prison. If only for your sake. You suffered enough in your life and I couldn't bear you to suffer me suffering all that terrible food. And shut up about my innocence. I will not hear of it. I will not believe that ridiculous, fantastic story that you overbalanced and broke your neck. You weren't the dying sort—" She seemed more relaxed now so he removed his hand from her lips.

He was about to continue talking but became aware that words were superfluous. She had suddenly acquired new tricks.

She could see right through him and there was no point in saying another word, so he sat cross-legged upon the floor and thought. He had to be honest. It wasn't only for her sake that he killed her.

Leah had been so happy during the night. What with Mr Fineberg and his gift of three bottles of vodka.

And even Aubrey had not been as suicidal as usual, despite the third of a bottle he had swallowed himself. He distinctly remembered lying upon the floor singing an Eskimo chant. He also remembered Auntie Beattie dancing the can-can on the table, revealing puce bloomers and green knotted knees. And then she knocked the goldfish bowl onto the floor, flushed the fish down the lavatory and tried to wear the empty bowl over her head.

"Take me to your leader," Aubrey remembered saying, and Auntie Beattie departed for her own home singing a Schubert love-song all the way down the street.

"Once a boy a rosebud found—roaming in the wildwood—"

He was sorry to see her go because now four bloodshot eyes scrutinised him.

"Isn't it time for your bed, young man?" Samuel Fineberg said as he winked and nudged him in the ribs.

"Yes, my Aubrey needs his sleep." Leah nodded as she washed and dried some glasses.

But he couldn't get up. His two longish legs had

probably caught the wasting disease of his pathetic middle leg, which he had kept well out of sight ever since—He did not wish to even utter Her name.

Fineberg helped him up and danced with him to the stairs.

"Aubrey! I can't let you go to bed with that beard," Leah shouted. "Change your beard, change your luck. It was the whiskers that caused you to be bad when you're good. Anyway, it don't look nice."

"I think it suits. Leave it. Live and let live." Fineberg sat down on a box and studied an empty coco-cola bottle with an expression of intense sorrow.

Aubrey could remember every minute detail with chronological precision. It was as if he were watching a private film played back especially for him.

"No one famous ever had a beard," Leah said, rushing round accumulating the necessary paraphernalia.

"What about Moses? Or Makarios or Leon Trotsky? They didn't do so bad."

"Leon Trotsky didn't do so good, either," Leah said as she approached her lolling lad with shaving head at the ready. "Be a lovely boy and let me remove your bumfluff."

Aubrey loathed her for that, for some unknown and incomprehensible reason. After all, it was not such an unreasonable request and he was quite ashamed of his feelings. So he rolled over, sunbathed under the glaring electric bulb, held in his fury and terrible hatred whilst Leah knelt above him, removing all traces of hair from his face, and all possibilities of fame in the future.

"Goodnight, Mr Fineberg," Leah said, without even turning to look at him.

"Goodnight? What do you mean, goodnight? The night is young; I'm not going yet."

"Yes, you are," Leah said, with finality.

[200]

"So I'm going," he shouted, and thumped to the door. "I'm going! I said I was going."

"So go," Leah replied. And Mr Samuel Fineberg, detective, went.

"You look much nicer now," Leah said, smiling down upon her son, stroking his chin. "And you see, your luck will change." She popped a sugared almond into his mouth and he felt very happy. She was a marvellous mother and he could not have her exposed to such dangerous men like Fineberg. It was at this precise moment that he decided to repay her for all her years of loving attention.

"Oy, I'm so tired," she said, stretching and creaking.

"Sit in this chair, Mother. I'll get you a pail of hot water to soak your feet."

She did what she was told and thus was relieved of the burden of having to live another sighing day longer.

Aubrey realised that he had thought the night away and yet another day had arrived.

He looked out of the window. Hessel Street was now full of people, and he wanted to get away from the street and house and shop and those evil jars of sweets. He wanted to get away from chocolate pyramids and give his mother a decent burial. But he did not want to escape from his guilt. Even though he did not want the world to know of it.

There was a loud rat-tat-tat on the shutters. It was not only unnecessary, it was also unusual.

"Open up! Open up in there," a voice of authority boomed.

Aubrey crouched to his knees and used Leah's body to shield his face from the shaking door.

Rat-tat-tat-tat.

He pressed his forehead against her exceptionally cold but rather smooth, reassuring skin.

"Open up in there! Open up in there!"

23

The music had to be faced, even the death march. So he walked slowly towards the door. He had not really expected to escape. She had said, "When I die, you'll die." No one could accuse him of not wanting to escape, but you couldn't get away from a woman like that.

He was about to throw open the door and reveal his nocturnal handicraft when he realised that the authoritative voice was owned by the face of Fineberg. "Is your mother up yet?"

"No, she's not up. She's down. And not as down as she's going to be." He chuckled for the benefit of his fate. "What have I got to lose?"

There was no reply. Fate had lost its tongue.

"When's Leah getting up? I must see her." Samuel Fineberg seemed very angry. "Where is she? We have certain objects to exchange," said the deprived detective, smiling to cover every twisted facet he owned. "Where is she? I can't wait."

"She's fast asleep. And she's going to be sleeping for some time." Aubrey stood against the door to make sure that it could not open more than an inch or two.

"Leah told me to come round. And have I got a bone to pick with her!"

"No shortage of bones, recently. Please, Fineberg, go away. My mother's head is splitting."

"I'll go when she pays me the seventy-five quid she owes me."

"Then she is better off where she is hiding," Aubrey replied. "I shall tell my mother when she awakes."

He tried to close the door but Fineberg went even redder than beetroot.

"I demand my fee. Or if not, at least she ought to marry me. She's got many things that belong to me. What's the point of sending invoices with the post these days? I'm coming back later for the soup she promised me."

The telephone rang. Aubrey slapped on a pained expression and managed to re-close the door on the little anguished face.

It was Auntie Beattie.

"Is your mother up?" The hysterical voice tumbled out of the other end.

"Sorry, Auntie. Mother isn't getting up today. She feels down in the dumps."

"Aubrey! Aubrey! You there? Put Leah on," Beattie demanded.

"Auntie darling! Mummy is resting, in absolute peace, and she cannot possibly be disturbed! She's very content but refuses to get up."

"I'm coming round. I'm coming round immediately," Auntie Beattie snapped.

"Wait a minute, Auntie, and I'll tell her." He held his hand over the receiver for a few moments, wondering what to do.

"What did she say?" Auntie Beattie called, but he didn't reply because he was still thinking.

"So, I'm coming. Shouldn't I, Aubrey?" Auntie Beattie shouted.

"Mother has a terrible head. She said come much later. She said she'll phone you first."

"Shouldn't wonder she's got a headache after all

that drink. Tell her I'm coming later. Tell her I'm waiting for her phone call."

"Yes," Aubrey replied.

He put down the 'phone and wondered what there was left for him to do.

No—maybe not the police. Why not the newspapers?

It would be nice for the world to understand the complex relationship that existed between a normal mother and son. Besides, the popular press would probably pay well, even though he could not accept one penny. But he dismissed the idea almost as soon as it occurred to him. There was really only one sensible thing to do; he had to get rid of Leah.

He went upstairs and in the wardrobe he found relics: the threadbare sealskin and fox-fur overcoats that had seen the funerals of Their Majesties King George the Fifth and the Sixth and the late Sir Winston Churchill, may he rest in peace, and Queen Mary, the Royal clockwork one. These coats had received all the waters of her wailing joy or despair, all the waters of a Whitechapel wife and a Whitechapel sky. They had had as many tears and mothballs as they could stand.

He rushed down the stairs with a bundle of her things wrapped up in her sequined wedding dress.

He would show Leah what true devotion could mean. He would dress her like a bride and send her off in style, even if the style wasn't exactly today's.

He rouged her cheeks and then covered her thin lips with her favourite lipstick. Now he carefully painted a delicate cupid's bow upon her mouth, superimposing it over her lips, thus making her mouth seem higher and fuller than the silly one she should never have been born with. He simply had to adorn her with care.

Now came the tricky part. He closed his eyes and removed her clothing, and because her mouth reeked

[204]

of drink he sprayed it with a rather spicy little perfume he had once picked up for her in Brighton.

Leah was lolling in the altogether, so Aubrey tried to keep his eyes closed as he pulled her wedding dress over her neck and body, until it covered the whole of her.

But before he could look at her there were still a few little tasks to accomplish. So he ripped the label from behind the neck of her wedding dress and twisted off her wedding ring and popped it into his trouser pocket. Then he removed her garish garnet solitaire from Fineberg and placed it upon his own finger. "Mmmm, rather nice!" But he wouldn't keep such a tasteless piece for long.

Aubrey looked around the house and seemed satisfied that there was only one other thing to do now.

"Dispose of the body. Oh yes. And just one thing more. Find a mad enough story to satisfy an hysterical sister and an avaricious, very sex-hungry, not so Fineberg."

Leah Feld simply had to disappear from off the face of the earth, or he would lose this new wonderful freedom that his mother had so generously given him.

He had to dispose of the little body of his mother, who for the first time in all his life he loved with all his heart, without one single reservation. And he would have to do it soon.

There simply had to be an answer. There would be an answer. Love would find a way.

24

The safe was very heavy, but bit by bit and by turning it on its corners, he managed to get it to the street door. Then he rested by sitting upon it.

His most dear mother had always insisted that only she knew the combination and—here was the irony —she had never failed to talk in her sleep and mumble those magic numbers, in proper order, night after night, ever since he could remember.

Aubrey made no bones about it, he had pressed his ear to her wall time and again, sometimes if only to reassure himself that she was still breathing. Fortunately she always had been—until now. But now was different. The way she looked was better than breathing.

He turned the squeaky metal knob to and fro and fro and to, and when the thick door opened he stuffed his pocket with pound notes and insurance policies. He was not disappointed to find such a small amount of ready cash. She was scared of burglars and trusted bank managers.

Then he surveyed the various stocks and shares certificates and wondered how he could transmute them into gold without Leah in the world to work the magic. Those tiring financial people always demanded one's actual physical presence to prove that one was still alive.

But he had no doubt that he would succeed.

Then he found something astonishing, right at the back of the safe: her last bank statement. It showed a balance of just over £10,000.

He had been sitting cross-legged on the floor, but he jumped up when he found yet more documents and digested them.

Aubrey hadn't known that Leah owned not only the house around him, but also the house next door.

No wonder Mr Ibrahim always smiled. He had to smile. Sub-letting four rooms and thereby getting rent from twenty people was not Commonwealth cricket, especially when there was no sub-letting clause.

So he removed everything of value and of possible value, which was everything, and wondered how to get the rest of that balance from that bank.

"But first things first." Aubrey rubbed his hands. He knew exactly what he had to do and whistled as he calculated the dimensions of the now empty safe. "To work! To work! Things to do."

Leah was very cooperative, for she emitted no noise whatsoever as he folded her up and shoved her inside the iron-wrought interior. She fitted splendidly and he was very pleased with her.

He stood back and admired the box. It was a solid piece of Victorian handiwork and it would last forever.

Nothing of Leah could possibly seep out and be dissipated upon the cold alien air. He felt extraordinarily close to her.

Opening the street door he wondered how to get the safe to the kerb, and once there, how to transport her to the river.

Mr Ibrahim saw him and flashed a smile.

"Ah, Ibrahim," he said in his best lord of the manor voice, "a moment, Ibrahim." Ibrahim came running.

Aubrey did not audibly request assistance but made a sweeping gesture with his two arms, from door to kerb, showing Ibrahim in balletic mime exactly what was required of him.

Ibrahim was not only kind enough to help, he almost fell over himself to shift the safe away from the house. Indeed, he pushed Aubrey out of the way. "No no, sir. You possibly get a rupture. I take your mother's safe-box."

Ibrahim did not stop smiling when he failed to push the safe away, but immediately gesticulated in an Asiatic tic-tac to his Pakistani chums, who dropped daughters, joss-sticks, garish rugs and cabbages to rush to Ibrahim, all of them flashing smiles as they groaned and pushed the safe, until it stood by the kerb.

Then the other Pakistanis returned to their customers, their wares, or their wives, but Ibrahim remained.

"Thank you, Ibrahim. Now I must remove this safe from here. I need transportation."

No sooner said than Ibrahim had gone and done. He returned with a market barrow and he shouted down the street. His friends came as quickly as before and with no less enthusiasm. It took six of them to lift the safe on to the barrow. It was very odd because his mother was such a small woman. True, he had had to bend her almost double to get her inside but that shouldn't have made a person any heavier. Possibly the Pakistanis were under-nourished.

"Yes, yes, old man. I simply must get this to a locksmith without delay."

Ibrahim, clever fellow that he was, knew that the audience was at an end. So he returned to earn his living and Aubrey pushed the barrow along Hessel Street and towards the river. It soared along. It practically ran away with him.

In Hessel Street all things were possible. Even if

Aubrey had carried out Leah's stiff carcass and dumped it into a dustbin, in full view of everyone, they would probably only have been interested in one thing. "One white Englishman now lived in that house, all alone. Perhaps he too will go to Paradise soon, Allah be praised." He could hear Ibrahim remarking this to one of his wives, the one he called his second eldest daughter.

Aubrey sang as he trotted along, for he was returning his mother to the River Thames from whence she had come, all those hungry years before. He was doing his duty. He was making a gesture to the God of his fathers. He was also showing that he was not laying up treasures upon the earth, because his greatest treasure, now inside the steel safe, would soon be under the sea and no longer on the wretched earth.

And he would be left with only her worldly fortune.

If only he could get away with it.

25

The riverside is never particularly busy on a Saturday afternoon, except for the gulls who do not have a union demanding a five-day week.

The entire area was deserted except for a few boys, but even they were on the other bank and therefore Aubrey felt perfectly safe.

The boys were throwing shoes into the river, probably to see who could throw the farthest. An occasional barge went by. And that was that. It was a beautiful yet forlorn scene, with the static giant cranes drooping towards their rippling reflections in the water.

One day he would retire from the world and paint and paint. People would come from the ends of the earth, just to watch him bespattered in the wind, snow and broiling sun, possessed only by the purpose of capturing the ever-changing poignant beauty of it all.

Sisley had not done too bad a job with the river. Neither had Turner. In fact both of them were quite above average in their approach. But Aubrey was sure that his own paintings in the Tate Gallery of the future would leave no doubt of his mastery and obsessive genius.

With these happy thoughts he tipped the barrow upward, and the safe containing his beautiful mother slid down over the parapet and splashed on the surface of the water.

When the splash had gone, so had Leah. The safe had gone straight down into the deeps, pushing up to the surface a beautiful display of bubbles. It was as if Leah was sending back a signal of thanks.

Any reasonable person would appreciate that this method of disposal was far nicer than being shoved under the earth, where worms and all manner of creeping crawlies started making a beeline for your liver and heart, by way of mouth, nostrils or earholes.

"Oh, Mother. Why have you left me?" Aubrey wailed. And he wept salt tears upon the sweet water. "Why have you left me all alone?"

He closed his eyes and clasped his hands together.

"Mother, hear me. What other son would go to such lengths, to such incredible trouble, to bring you to the end that only you deserve? My respect for you is limitless. Sometimes I nearly weakened, saying to myself, 'Let her live on and suffer. Let her live on even if she is alone, even if her friends have gone.' But my respect and love for you always conquered my weakness. And so you are here. But knowing you, the sands of time will shift you gradually, gradually. For who could hold you back? You'll move slowly—towards the sea. You'll go slowly, following my tears, across the ocean, back to Russia, across the seas back to Odessa, back to where you came from. And I, Aubrey Field, have made this possible. Amen."

He threw several kisses at the water, turned and walked away from her, for ever and ever and ever.

Aubrey pushed the barrow away from the riverside and along deserted streets.

"I'm afraid. I'm so afraid," he wailed.

"What did you say?" An old man in a doorway looked across at him with astonishment.

"I didn't say anything," Aubrey shouted back over his shoulder.

He had to get away from these streets, these unreal, grimy streets, these empty streets clogged with ghosts and memories, deserted by the children of Israel, but thick with the loitering souls of their bronchial parents.

And he knew he was afraid. Afraid of today and tomorrow, afraid of being alone, and afraid of Auntie Beattie who would drive him mad in no time at all.

The market barrow hurtled homeward, but he was afraid of the eye of tomorrow staring down from the sky, and the eye of the present peeping up through the floorboards or down through the ceiling, or the eyes that watched him from the other side of the mirror.

Aubrey made up his mind that he would never again look in a mirror just in case he wasn't there. For it suddenly dawned upon him. How did you prove that you were you, if there was no one around to recognise and speak to you?

And he was afraid of the black, yellow and brown people who would take over the world. There would be only dark faces in Hessel Street from now on to watch over him, until his face disappeared completely.

As he entered Hessel Street, he ran along like the boy he was only a few weeks before.

Ibrahim was not by his stall, which was strange, because on Saturday Ibrahim never left his stall. But the stall itself wasn't there, neither were all the other stalls.

Now this was really strange, because it was Saturday and market day. But when he gazed up at the sky, he realised he had spent more hours by the river with his dearest mother than he had imagined.

"And why not?" he explained to an intelligent-looking cat. "Why not? Didn't she sacrifice her life for me? Didn't she die in order that I could get rid of her?"

The cat mewed, "Aubrey! You're dead right."
Then it shot away.

He leaned against the grey wall.

"Sweet-shop opening soon, mister?"

He looked down. A child with eyes as huge as Jaffa
oranges stared up at him.

"You Indians look so beautiful, so Jewish," he said,
stroking her hair. "What did you say, bubeller?"

"Sweet-shop opening soon, mister?" she repeated in
exactly the same tone. These words were practically
the first that the children of Hessel Street learned.
They took up the lollipop as soon as they put down
the nipple.

"Soon. Soon." He nodded, and the child ran away
happily.

But he still could not go inside, for Leah was not in
there, not even the spirit of her. For as soon as he had
folded her up and put her inside the safe, she had gone
from the face of the earth, for ever. It was a lonely
Leahless world.

One could live without love, one could somehow
struggle through without hating a single soul, one
could even survive without Zena, but how could one
live without a loving mother whom you hated with
all your heart and soul and might?

How could he live without a quarrel every morning, afternoon and evening? He needed to be constantly
nagged and harried and reminded how terrible everything was, is and would be.

He needed the abrasive tongue of a tyrant mother.
He needed to live with the full knowledge of failure
and futility.

Aubrey entered the empty house and was catapulted
back to the world when he heard the telephone ringing.

As he went to answer it he tried to avoid his reflec-

tion in the discoloured mirror. But he could not resist the stark eyes of the beardless nonentity who stared
back at him.

Then he answered the 'phone.

26

It was Auntie Beattie. Who else?

"I've been 'phoning for hours and there's been no answer." Beattie sounded quite demented. Not having been able to contact Leah by Diaspora Umbilica had thrown her into a form of panic unknown even to her.

"There has been no answer because the 'phone has been out of order." Aubrey spoke each word slowly, placing it into the mouthpiece with the precision of a picador.

"Nonsense! I had it checked by the engineers. I even spoke to the supervisor. Where's Leah? What's going on?"

"Mother's gone. Her train arrived in Bournemouth half an hour ago."

"Bournemouth?" Beattie spluttered the name of the fair resort with such vehemence that she might have been referring to Berlin or Cairo. "Bournemouth? Why Bournemouth? She's only just come back."

"Yes, Auntie Beattie. And she's gone back there again."

"What's happening at Bournemouth? Something's up? What's she getting up to at Bournemouth? All my blood is chilled suddenly. So what about the shop?"

"I'm looking after the shop."

"You'll lose all the customers!"

"I said I'm looking after it."

"That's what I mean. Something fishy is going on."

"Bye-bye, Auntie Beattie. Must dash. A customer."

But no one was in the shop because he had locked the door. And it would stay locked.

"What hotel is Leah staying at?" Beattie demanded. "She's obviously suffering from a brainstorm. An attack of Aubreyitis, if you don't mind me being personal, Aubrey."

"I am not quite sure which hotel." His mind was spinning.

"It can only be one of the eighteen leading hotels. She'd only stay at one of the top-grade kosher ones. I'll 'phone all of them. I don't like it. I'll find out and 'phone you back. Something's going on." She sounded like a siren crying for the end of the world.

And thus, with a mission in life, Auntie Beattie replaced her receiver in order to telephone eighteen leading kosher hotels. Aubrey was left alone again, and he savoured the moment.

He realised that every nightmare had another side. The world was Leahless, but on the other hand he had never experienced being really alone before, except in the lavatory. Even there she used to call, "Aubrey! Don't fall down the hole."

He was certain of one thing: he would not panic. Panic, induced by lack of confidence, brought about self-destruction. Therefore panic was simply the first stage of suicide. And even though he had a high regard for the kingdom of death, he was not in the slightest bit attracted to the idea of immediate suicide.

He would survive by taking a leaf out of the book of the ancient Chinese—he would bend with the wind. This way he would not snap or be broken by the mediocre machine of the Metropolitan Police.

Not that he did not admire the average policeman.

The London police had a thankless task keeping the streets safe from perverts and arsonists. Indeed, his regard for them knew no bounds, and his admiration extended from the humble constable to the Home Secretary himself.

He quickly jumped under the table and crouched on all fours, not because the bell suddenly rang, but because he had once read in a book about Passion, published in Calcutta, that crouching low in this manner during times of stress helped to evolve a means of individual thinking and non-involvement in seemingly impossible situations.

And of course he was quite aware that the bell had rung.

His means of individual thinking led him to two questions. Firstly: "Who is at the door?" Secondly: "What the hell am I to do now?"

He was definitely not overwrought. If anything he was underwrought.

To pace on your knees backwards and forwards, head horizontal on neck, two hands tugging handfuls of remaining hair was not panic but just another means of standing back from the picture show called life.

The bell rang and rang.

He mocked his reflection. "It tolls for thee."

He had lost all respect for the imposter in the mirror. "But not for me."

He got up and went to the door.

"Who is it?" he called through the wood, allowing not a shred of urgency into his voice.

"It's me. Fineberg. Sometimes called the Private Oy. Aubrey! Let me in."

Aubrey opened the door an inch or two.

Fineberg tried to see over Aubrey's head. This was not very easy, as he wasn't as tall as Aubrey, not even on tiptoe.

"My mother's gone to Bournemouth, Hampshire. She left in a hurry. It was a man I believe."

Fineberg riposted with the laugh of a man who had nothing to fear from rivals. "Ridiculous. She invited me to soup, last night. Tell your mother I'm exhausted, so she doesn't have to run away from me any more."

"Sorry, no dice, Fineberg."

"Be a friend. Be reasonable and I'll make it worth your while."

"Sorry. Mother has fled from Tower Hamlets." He managed to close the door but Fineberg on the other side shouted, "I smell some rats and I don't like it. I will return in one hour. If your mother does not receive me in the manner which I am getting used to, I will pursue my own enquiries. Which could mean the police."

"What are you trying to get at, Fineberg? Who, or rather whom are you accusing? And of what?" Aubrey opened the window and spoke to the back of the man, who still stood nose pressed against the door. The detective turned and smiled.

"Not accusing you of anything. God forbid. But Aubrey, listen, I can't understand Leah rushing off to Bournemouth. That is, if she did. And I see no reason why I shouldn't believe you. Toodleloo."

He turned to go, but shouted up to the window where once she had sighed away her darkened hours with Turkish delight. "Leah! Listen! You can be a full partner in my agency. No strings. Just marriage."

Then he turned to Aubrey. "Yes, a full partner." He laughed from his belly. "A full sleeping partner, of course," he added. "Get the joke? Mind you, who's going to sleep?" He shrugged at Aubrey. "I'm human, only human, I'm afraid."

"Thanks for telling me."

Aubrey watched him go. "See you in an hour,"

Fineberg shouted back without turning around. Smoke swirled up all around him as he puffed his pipe.

Aubrey noticed that Fineberg either had gigantic holes in his socks or that he wasn't wearing any socks at all.

27

He was lying with his cheek pressed to the tablecloth when the 'phone rang again. This time he did not crouch down or spring up. It could only be Auntie Beattie.

Her voice was more subdued. "I 'phoned every hotel, every first-class kosher hotel in Bournemouth, and Leah's not in any of them."

"Maybe she's signed in under an assumed name."

But she had not even heard his reply. "If she's not home by the time I come there I'm calling the police. And, what's more, I'm coming by taxi."

So the end had come. There was simply no point in trying to escape the inevitable. As his dear departed mother had constantly reminded him, God rest her dear soul, "If you're destined to drown, Aubrey, you will in a soup-spoon." There was nothing to do except wait. Everything was tidy, so there was no need to feel ashamed when the house filled with policemen and photographers.

He resumed his previous posture, burying his head in his folded arms. "Anyway, there's no point in living. She was right when she said, 'When I die you will die'."

He hadn't realised until now how prophetic all her utterances had been. And only now could he see what a loss she was to the human race. Only now did he realise how she must have suffered at the hands of her most ungrateful son who had despatched her in her late prime.

Too late he could see how much he owed to Leah the Felled. He would give himself up with all the nobility he could muster.

If only it were possible to reverse the situation. If only Leah were alive and having to face the lone battle, to which only she was truly equal. Aubrey was pleased that at least he had the courage to admit that he was not all strength this day. And he knew that, despite his sorrow and remorse, the selfish desire for self-preservation would prevail. "Dear Mother, forgive me! How vulnerable I am."

She would forgive him, but he knew he would never forgive himself for this last desperate attempt to get off the hook.

He decided to open the shop, for if life was as sweet as Jewish sages claimed, children certainly should not be deprived of the sugar that made it so. Anyway, it wasn't nice to run away leaving an empty till. "Aubrey Field felled Leah Feld for all the property she held." He would pass into folklore.

"Two ice lollies and three strips of bubble-gum."

"Yes, dear. One and three please. Hey! You! Got a rocket to catch? Rascal! Take your turn. Listen, Ismael, do me a favour, when the sword of the Prophet smites the world again, remember how kind Uncle Aubrey was. Come on, in front. I'll serve you first."

"Sherbet dab. A sherbet dab. Want a sherbet dab."

He would wait for Auntie Beattie before beating it to Dusseldorf. Yes! Brilliant! Whoever thought of looking for anyone in Dusseldorf—except Dusseldorfers seeking other Dusseldorfers. It was the last place in the world to look for anyone or anything.

But perhaps he would wait for the bank to open on Monday and forge her signature once again.

"Mister, please, what about my sherbet dab?"

His hands and eyes roamed over the rows of ha' penny delights, but the sherbet dabs eluded him.

"Where's your mummy? She knows where they are," a little girl said, her hands clutched between her fidgety legs, wanting to wee-wee.

"Not in the shop, dear. Wait till you get back to your own floor."

"I'm terribly sorry," he told another little face, "you know as well as I do I can't serve you cigarettes. Come back in nine years' time."

The children went out giggling. He closed the door behind them and awaited Auntie Beattie, who was now flying towards him in a taxi, no doubt watching with horror the price mounting on the meter.

He felt ravenous, so he cut himself a slice of bread, covered it with a thick layer of smoked cod's roe and devoured it. Then he heard the taxi.

Aubrey opened the door without waiting for Auntie Beattie to reach it, and she rushed in flushed with anger. "That man, I'll report him."

"I watched, Auntie. He was a lowlife."

"What do you mean, lowlife? He was lower. I gave him a whole sixpence for himself and he threw it back at me. Where's your mother? I must see her. I know she's here."

He paused before replying and sucked his finger. Then he realised that the same finger held the garnet ring.

He placed his hand behind his back, and as he paced the shop he tugged at the ring, but it would not come off.

"Where is she? She's ill. Say something. Poor Aub! You seem too shocked to speak. She's not on the danger list, is she? Which hospital? Oh my poor Leah! Speak! I'm your Auntie, I deserve to know."

But still he could not reply. She clutched the flesh of his arms. "I know. Don't tell me. She's lost. She fell down and lost her mind and she's wandering somewhere—" She went straight to the telephone. "Don't worry, Aubrey. The police will help us because she's done them many favours. How many cups of tea? I've lost count. I'll dial 999."

He rushed forward to stop her, but realised that the restraining hand carried his mother's bauble. He quickly withdrew his hand and withered it up into his sleeve.

Auntie Beattie started to dial the three numbers that would take him away from the world.

28

He heard a female answer at the other end and he quickly jumped forward. "It's all right. Mother's upstairs."

"Oh, that's all right, dear," Auntie Beattie cooed into the receiver at the girl in Scotland Yard. "Sorry to have bothered you." She replaced the receiver and sighed with relief.

"Why is she upstairs? What's wrong with her? Why did she come back from Bournemouth?"

"She didn't go. She went to the station, but decided to go to a news theatre instead. She's lying down now, recovering from the news. And me!"

"She's always recovering from you. I'm going up."

But Aubrey barred her way to the stairs with wide open arms. "I'll go upstairs and tell her you're here. Please sit down, Auntie, and have a nice cup of tea, and I'll get her to come down. You just sit there and rest your veins."

She looked at him with delight. "You always were my favourite nephew."

"I'm your only nephew."

"So you are. I get so confused these days. Yes, I will sit down. Thank God someone's got consideration." Auntie Beattie slumped into upholstery and enjoyed the rare luxury of attention.

Aubrey rushed up the stairs to the room where his mother was not, all the while tugging the ring on his finger. "Evidence!" It would not budge.

But now he knew what he had to do. He would go to his mother's room, jump out of the window and never be seen again by anyone.

He dashed towards the window and looked through the glass at the street below. It was all so simple. He would throw it open and jump.

But there was one snag. It was fixed firmly with nails. Leah hated fresh air. She said it was bad for the complexion.

Auntie Beattie was pounding the door. She hadn't trusted him and had followed him up.

There was no way out.

"Leah! Leah! Are you all right? Leah! Speak to me."

He had no choice. "I'm fine. See you soon." Aubrey was pleased with his imitation of Leah's voice. If he hadn't sent her on such a long excursion, they could easily have earned a living touring the music-halls, she the stuffed doll, screwing around her scrawny neck, he making her move and speak with ever-increasing perfection.

"Leah! Let me in. I must talk to you. Let me in or I'll break the door down. Leah—!"

Beattie had no more bulk than Leah but she tended to get over-emotional.

"I mean it! I'll smash the door down with my behind if necessary."

Aubrey quickly grabbed his mother's silk scarf, tied it around his head, and pulled her astrakhan coat over his huddled body.

"Let me in, Leah. I don't care what you're doing. I must see you in the flesh."

So far Beattie's words had not spilled over into action, and Aubrey felt he just had time to squirt some eau-de-Cologne over himself. So he did this, and then for a final touch he rouged his cheeks and cupid-bowed his lips.

He was ready now, and, although he was wearing trousers and needed a shave, he reckoned that he could pass Auntie Beattie's scrutiny.

He sighed and sighed to get inside the role, and then he opened the door.

Auntie Beattie fell upon him. "Oh, Leah. I was so worried about you! Please don't choke me off. I know I worry for nothing, but I thought something terrible had happened to you."

"Beattie, Beattie, darling Beattie! Do me a favour. You're such a silly girl! Have I had a terrible time with Aubrey! He's driven me mad. After all I did for him and he suddenly gives me such aggravation. Only you know what I go through."

"Of course I know. I'm your sister. I care enough to want to know. Where is he?" Beattie peered round the room through the perpetual fog of her eyes. "Where's Aubrey? Didn't he come in here?"

"He came and went! For always. To Israel. I gave him the money to get rid of him. If I never see him again that may be too soon. Matter of fact I'm pretty sure we'll never see poor Aubrey again."

"You've got nothing to blame yourself for, Leah."

"Who's blaming myself? Why say such a stupid thing? Anyway, how are you today?"

"You are asking me how I am, Leah? I'm feeling terrible. Thank you for asking me."

Auntie Beattie lost her melancholy and gazed at her sister with gratitude.

"Beattie! Now that Aubrey's gone, everything will be like old times. We were such lovely friends. Remember? Remember playing hospitals? And me letting you sometimes hold my dolly? Remember? And how I let you play sometimes with my friends?"

Auntie Beattie smiled and nodded and tears rolled down her cheeks, following well-watered paths.

Leah's words were a long overdue miracle.

Then Auntie Beattie peered very close. "You're so lovely, Leah. Never seen you look so lovely. Wish I was so lovely."

"So do I," he replied. He knew just what to say. He knew just the right method to make Beattie happy and grateful.

Then the doorbell rang and Aubrey knew it was Fineberg. He went downstairs following his stumbling myopic Auntie.

He opened the door slightly. "What do you want?" he croaked at the little man.

Fineberg peered over Aubrey's shoulder. This time it was possible, because Aubrey was lower than usual, bending his back and also his knees. He wanted Fineberg to see his performance of Leah, with Auntie Beattie in the gloom of the living-room, secure once again in the sanctuary of her melancholia. "What do you want, Fineberg?" he shouted again.

"I want you. I mean I want soup. You promised me soup."

"You bore me, Fineberg. Go." Aubrey slammed the door.

"I want my money for locating your son," Fineberg added through the door.

"Give him the money and get rid of him," Auntie Beattie said.

"Give me my fee, my fee." Fineberg's voice rose from the depths of anger to a tentative pleading. "I must get my fee. Please."

Aubrey thrust his hand into his trouser pocket and then stuffed four fivers through the letter-box. "Take them and go out of my life."

"Twenty? There's only twenty," Fineberg moaned.

"That's all you're getting. Now go."

Aubrey signalled his aunt to remain silent as he heard the detective jump up and down on the pavement outside. "My fee! My fee. You owe me another fifty-five." Nevertheless the voice got weaker and weaker until it vanished entirely, and Aubrey peeped out of the window and he saw Fineberg just before he disappeared around a corner.

Aubrey turned to Auntie Beattie with a deep ancestral sigh. "Oy, I've had such a day. But he's gone. At last."

Beattie was so happy that she was even prepared to go. "I'm overjoyed that you got rid of that terrible man. I was so afraid of him. You know, Leah, I never imagined things. Well—you have no idea what he used to try to do to me when you weren't looking. I said *tried* to. In corridors. Under the table. Everywhere."

"I'll see you to the bus, Beattie dear."

Beattie did not faint, because the day had been simply crammed with such surprises. "Leah, I must say, you haven't been so nice as this for years. I feel like crying."

"You always needed a lot of love, Beattie. Unfortunately that boy of mine drove me mad. He sucked all my energy. But thank God he's settled now, so I can concentrate on helping you to overcome your melancholic moments. One day you'll even be slightly happy, Beattie. You'll see. Lots of things are going to change from now on."

"You're too good to me."

"I know. I'm too good to everyone. That's my weakness. Hold on, Beattie. Won't be a moment. Must go somewhere where no one can go for me."

Aubrey went to the lavatory, rolled up his trouser legs, pulled the chain, and returned to the street door. "Yes, I'll enjoy a nice walk to the main road."

They left the house, holding each other's arms and leaning together. As they slowly progressed towards the bus-stop, even from behind you could see that they were the sole survivors of that extinct race called Jews who once populated these shores. You could prove this quite easily by the way they stopped every so often to take a deep breath and expel it with a sigh.

29

On his way back home Aubrey found it impossible to go at his usual speed. He tried, but his legs simply would not obey him. The pace was exactly the same as the stroll to the bus-stop with Beattie. "Lovely person, Beattie. One in a million," he said to himself.

If only he could have got back to the house sooner, he would have felt happier. It wasn't safe to be alone in the streets these days. And that front door seemed such a long way away, and there were so many windows and doorways with such dark thoughts within them.

True, faithful Ibrahim was smiling from the other end of the street, but every solitary man was looking towards him. "Dirty beasts!"

They had never looked so much at him before. His thoughts tenderly flew to his mother in the deep. She was a great lady, and certainly she had had enough trouble with all these sex maniacs around.

"What do they want of my life? I'm not that attractive, am I? They say that even a middle-aged lady ain't safe any more. I don't know what the world's coming to." Yet, like Leah, he loved this street. It was better than anywhere else. "So wonderful to be amongst your own. But how can you leave Hessel Street and start all over again, if you have regular customers? Believe me! Don't you think I would? I bought a lovely bit of beef for boiling. I'm all alone in the world. Where can I go?"

Everything he knew had been born and had breathed and had died and was buried in this street. He would never get away from this street.

"Good evening, Mrs Feld," Mr Ibrahim said as Aubrey approached.

Aubrey nodded, allowing just one flick of smile to escape his lips, an exact reproduction of his mother's. Then he went inside.

At last he was alone.

Loneliness wasn't nice but being alone was wonderful. And from now on there would be no one to talk to except Beattie. But she was no one.

Beattie went through one ear and came out the other.

There was no one to talk to, no one to nag, no one to be nagged by. He could talk to himself, but that was quite different.

The other Aubrey had jumped out of the window and was safely tucked away in Israel and dead to the Diaspora. Israel had claimed another son. Perhaps he had been killed in a skirmish, bravely. Who would have imagined that Aubrey Field, who promised so well and who was thwarted, would eventually die for Zion and be awarded the highest medal for bravery, posthumously? It just showed that you couldn't tell how a person would turn out. Alone and single-handed he had saved a kibbutz by drawing the fire. He started to sing the melodious minor-key Hebrew national anthem. "Kol—od be—le—vav p'ni—ma—" He sang the words of the one line he remembered; strange sounds which he felt but did not understand. He hummed his way through the rest of the plaintive tune, and when he reached the end he cried and looked out of the window.

The faces he once knew would always keep coming. They would come through and sit around the radio and play cards. They would keep on returning, all those old faces that he thought had gone for ever.

But the face of Aubrey would never return. What was the point of Aubrey returning? What sort of future could he have? Better Leah than Aubrey. What was the point of Aubrey?

"Lovely boy. Difficult but lovely. Better off dead in the holy land," he said, gazing out at the street. "Imagine, Aubrey a hero. Fallen for his people. Dead but remembered. Outnumbered in a skirmish. Clean through his head. Brain exploded."

Soon he would do some washing-up and a bit of sewing and bit of baking. And then watch the telly for a bit. And then go to bed. And tomorrow open the shop. Always so much to do."

Yes. He would make a little drop of soup, and scrape the carrots and singe the chicken, peel a big onion, and slide it all into the salty water, with the giblets. And while all that was simmering nicely, he would start cooking the Rakusen's egg vermicelli and skimming the scum off the soup's surface at the same time. There was always so much to do.

And Aubrey? What did he have? He didn't have memories even, nor faith, nor even ambition, just mad dreams. You can't survive with mad dreams. "Mad dreams don't pay for cheesecake or candles."

The only thing you could do with mad dreams was to die and disappear, or to run up a mountain against an invisible enemy and impossible odds and get those dreams taken care of.

So he had; and had been been given a medal to prove how mad he was. And now they called him a hero, which was just another name for madman.

And when they spoke about him and the crazy action that caused life to dribble out of the holes that the bullets made, they never cried but laughed—but nicely.

"Still, he probably did a sensible thing. If you ain't got a future, and you ain't got a past, what's the point of surviving?"

Suddenly he knew he loved the past. The past did not grow old. The past left you alone and made no demands on you. You couldn't change the past. It was far, far better to be Leah in the past than to be Aubrey with no future.

He went to the kitchen and gathered the bread-crumbs into one heap with the breadknife. "Yes Aubrey! You're better off gone. I can rely on you now you're dead. Brave boy! Every mother should sacrifice such a bit of flesh for Zion."

The past was authentic because they had photos to prove it, and furniture and tombstones, and insurance policies. The past was warm and cosy; but who would like to bet upon the future? Who could trust that it would even put in an appearance for any respectable length of time?

He started scraping the carrots. "You can live on nice soup and happy memories, believe me."

Aubrey was happy tonight. He put on the soup and soon it was simmering nicely, and the lokshen was on and everything was under control. There was always so much to do.

He drew the curtains, laid the fire, lit it and blew up the smoking firewood until the flames roared up the chimney.

"Yes, Aubrey's better off dead. Why should I feel guilty? I sent him to his people. Should I now die of grief? Why should I? I'm not the dying sort; besides, I've got my shop to run and my rents to collect. What can you do when your son closes his eyes, because he doesn't want to face that there's no place for him in a world with no future? He just rots under the ground, his skull grinning. 'I'm a hero.' I'm something at last. Now leave me alone. And if you must speak about me say only nice things. So now what can you do with such a lovely meshuggener?"

He dabbed powder on his face. It filled the room and flew everywhere.

"On with the motley, the paint and the powder," he sang but soon swapped the deep voice for the high tones of Mimi. "They—call me—mi—mi—"

He sucked his lip and poked his tongue out at the reflection. "All right! If you know of another face— if you have an alternative—" The reflection stayed silent.

He switched on the telly, switched it off just as fast, then went to the radio where they were playing music of yester-year. That took him back. "You are my honey, honey-suckle, I am the bee . . ."

He danced into the kitchen, prepared the strudel and put it into the oven; then he danced back to the living-room, where he slumped down into the chair, looked into his compact, refurbished his Leah face, and waved his tired forefinger to keep in time with the songs that they did not seem to make so well these days, days that are simply not worth thinking about.

"Forward! Everyone talks about going forward! Politicians! Teenagers! Scientists! Artists! Everyone's looking forward."

Now he was talking to Leah in the mirror. "What's so wonderful about forward? Forward to where? Forward to the future? What's so wonderful about the future? The good old days. Now you're talking!"

He stood up, waltzed a little and hokey-cokeyed, poured himself some cherry brandy, and argued with the ceiling.

"Hitler? What are you talking about? How can you blame the past for Hitler? Hitler was the future, the beginning of it. And Aubrey is the past. God bless him."

If only one could retrieve the past, retrace one's steps. It was all there. "You can't beat a nice Yiddisher home with candles. Even if you do forget the meaning of why you lit them."

He lit the candles even though it wasn't Friday night. "What difference? Who cares? Is God going to come and tell me off? I've got plenty to tell him also."

No one would come, and he was glad. God, like Mr Fineberg, would not come to visit her in Hessel Street. No one would ever come with the answer. No one could sell her strudel in the sky.

She poured liquid the colour and consistency of blood, but nice blood, liquid she had made herself. She lifted the glass. "To my lovely Aubrey. Outnumbered, alone, he went back to defend his people. To Aubrey! A hero! Lochaim." She raised her glass to her child lost in the dark and sipped her home-made cherry brandy slowly. When the glass was drained she stuck her tongue down into it, so as to extract the full sweetness from the last drop. Then she got up and went towards her kitchen where the food was cooking very nicely. Somewhere perhaps in the past there was an answer, but even if there was not it didn't matter. The smell was absolutely delicious.

No. She wanted strudel on earth. While she had hands to bake it and nostrils to smell it and a mouth to eat it. After all, you can't beat a nice piece of strudel, if you make it according to the recipe.

When you summed up everything, from the beginning of life to the end, you had to admit that despite the terrible difficulties and whether you believe in God or not, God was good. And life was exceptionally sweet. She knew exactly where everything was and was pleased that now there was nobody else in the house to move things. "Yes, killed defending his people. So I

[235]

suppose I'll never see him again," she said quite happily.

Leah skimmed the scum from the surface of the soup, breathed in deeply and stirred and stirred with her very old and extra-large wooden ladle, the sort you couldn't buy nowadays, not for love nor money. She stirred the steaming golden liquid round and around and the music played in the other room.

"Lovely fowl," she said, "and so many eggs! It'll last me the whole week."

Then she slowly bent down on to her knees, sighed and opened the oven and looked at the lovely strudel that was slowly browning to perfection.

The reassuring smell of the chicken soup hovered on the air, cancelling out everything else, and Leah Feld, her ladle cradled within her folded arms, could not remember another time in all her life when she had been so happy.

Milton Keynes UK
Ingram Content Group UK Ltd.
UKHW011324030324
438845UK00001B/78

9 780393 337372